Enchanting the Bear

RAYNA TYLER

3

ALSO BY RAYNA TYLER

Seneca Falls Shifters

Tempting the Wild Wolf
Captivated by the Cougar
Enchanting the Bear
Enticing the Wolf
Teasing the Tiger

Ketaurran Warriors

Jardun's Embrace
Khyron's Claim
Zaedon's Kiss
Rygael's Reward
Logan's Allure

Crescent Canyon Shifters

Engaging His Mate
Impressing His Mate

CHAPTER ONE

BRYSON

"Believe me Bear, I know how you feel." Just looking at the quills protruding from the swollen flesh on the side of the dog's muzzle made me cringe.

I'd been a cub, barely accomplishing shifts on my own without assistance, when I'd encountered my first porcupine. I knew firsthand what kind of pain having the skin punctured on your face could cause. I'd have thought after the last time Mandy brought the dog to see Mitch Jacobson, the local vet, he would have learned his lesson and left the prickly animals alone.

I guess some of life's lessons are harder to learn than others, even for natural-born animals.

The dog thumped his tail on the truck's leather seat, then whimpered. A noise I'd sympathetically endured for the umpteenth time during the drive from the lodge of the Seneca Falls Resort to Mitch's neighboring home. I stretched out my arm, avoiding the cluster of sticklike protrusions, then scratched him behind the ears.

I glanced at the newly constructed entrance on the side of Mitch's house. I'd heard he recently converted a portion of his home into an office by adding a moderate sized reception area near the spare bedroom he used as an exam room. Normally, anyone in need of his services during the week would have to drive all the way to Ashbury. With the new office opened on Saturday morning, those of us who lived nearby didn't have to make the long drive down the mountain. Fortunately for Bear, it was the beginning of the weekend and Mandy had called ahead to make an appointment.

The last time I'd been here was when Berkley, Nick's sister, had been out running in her wolf form and gotten shot by a guy hired by the psychotic girlfriend of an ex-boyfriend. It was a good thing Mitch was one of the few humans in the area who knew about shifters. He'd saved her life and earned the gratitude of her family, her mate, and me.

There was only one other car parked near the entrance, so I figured we wouldn't have long to wait. "Let's get this over with." I made my way around the truck, then lifted the dog off the seat and cradled him in my arms. Most male bear shifters were big guys, and I was no different. I could have easily tucked the dog under one arm.

I hadn't even made it two steps when Bear's pitiful whimpers vocalized into louder moans. I didn't care what anybody said, dogs were smart. He knew where we were, why we were here, and wasn't happy about it. "Sorry, bud. You'll feel a lot better once Mitch takes those out." I pressed on the metal bar across the middle of the glass door and stepped inside.

"Good morning." A female I'd never met before was sitting behind the reception desk. "You're here for an appointment, right?"

"Yes, I—I…" Why was I stuttering? I was a man of few words, believed in getting straight to the point in most situations, but I never had a problem forming sentences. And I never, ever stuttered.

Maybe it had something to do with the fact that I'd

been holding my breath from the moment my gaze locked with those dark eyes the color of ripened acorns. Or maybe it was because she had the most radiant smile I'd ever seen on a female and it had my heart revving faster than an expertly tuned engine in a race car.

I sucked in air, then gulped again when my lungs didn't respond right away.

"Mitch is finishing up with his last patient, so it should only be a few more minutes." She glanced at the computer screen on the desk in front of her. "Will you need shots today as well?" She tapped a few keys.

"Why would I need shots?" I asked, distractedly paying more attention to the way her soft brown curls framed her face and the subtle hint of lavender in her scent than to her actual question.

"I was talking about your dog, Bear."

Being a male who could shift into a bear, I always found it amusing every time I heard the animal's name spoken out loud. I couldn't figure out if Nick, Mandy's mate and the dog's owner, was trying to be humorous or if he thought his pet really did resemble one of my kind. Though how an animal with mangy brown fur and a body that was longer than his legs came close to looking like a bear, I wasn't sure. "He's not my dog."

"He's not?" Suspicion furrowed her brow. "I could have sworn when Mandy was in a few weeks ago, she said he belonged to her fiancé…" She pointed at the screen. "I'm sorry, aren't you Nick Pearson?"

"No, I-I'm…" I stammered. Again. What was wrong with me? Why couldn't I make what I said sound coherent? It wasn't as if I had a problem articulating or talking to females. I talked to the women who worked at the resort all the time. So why did this particular female with the full, kissable lips have my tongue sticking to the roof of my mouth? And why was my bear, normally bored and uninterested in most females, suddenly rumbling and urging me to get closer to this one?

"Nick's my boss. My name is Bryson, Bryson Cruise." My voice sounded deeper and more gravelly than usual, thanks to my bear, but at least my tongue was no longer paralyzed.

She rolled her chair away from the desk and walked around to my side of the counter. "Nice to meet you. I'm Leah." Her gaze flashed to the Seneca Falls logo on my shirt. "Do you work at the resort?"

"Security." Though lately, my job description had taken on new parameters. With Mandy and Nick's upcoming wedding, I'd gone from patrolling the property and keeping it safe to idea consultant for their new house, cake taste tester—no complaints on that task—and finally doggy caretaker. Since Mandy and Nick had a meeting with the contractor this morning regarding final changes to their new home, they'd asked me if I wouldn't mind taking care of Bear.

The dog was back to whimpering pathetically, which was fine with me because it encouraged Leah to remain standing next to me.

"Poor thing. You've been playing with that nasty porcupine again, haven't you?" She swept her hand along Bear's flank, her fingertips grazing my arm. Her skin was warm, soft, soothing. So soothing that my animal was insisting I shift so he could rub all over her. Hell, I was ready to forgo seeing Mitch, toss her over my shoulder, and take her back to my house.

The females I'd been attracted to in the past, the ones I'd shared an occasional bed with, had all been shifters. None of them came close to eliciting the kind of response I was experiencing with this human. My inability to think, my straining cock—currently concealed by Bear—and my animal's overwhelming desire to claim could only mean one thing.

"Hey, Bryson." It took a lot to startle me, to make me jump, but having Mitch stroll into the reception area during my moment of revelation was enough to do it.

I grunted a response, too afraid to attempt a conversation.

He took one look at Bear and shook his head. "I'll be right with you." Then he stepped aside to make room for the elderly woman who'd followed him out of the exam room carrying a plaid blanket wrapped around a black-and-gray-striped cat. It was Alma Chapman. I'd known the female most of my life. She was old when I was a teenager and had to be at least eighty or older now.

"Bryson. You make sure to tell your mother I said hello next time you see her." She waggled a decrepit finger at me, then dismissed me completely as she headed for Mitch and the open door he was holding for her.

"Make sure you bring her back in two weeks." Mitch scratched the cat's head.

"I won't forget, promise," Alma said, smiling at Mitch as if he possessed magical healing powers.

Mitch closed the door and said, "I see you've met my *sister*, Leah."

Sister? What? It was then that I noticed the slight family resemblance. Funny how learning certain tidbits of information could cool a raging erection.

"Ignore him. He's been using the big-brother intimidation technique on every good-looking guy I've met since high school." Leah winked, then patted my arm, sending tingles skittering across my skin.

I couldn't tell if her teasing was out of politeness or an insinuation that she found my appearance appealing.

I was, however, concerned my discovery would change my relationship with Mitch. He was a friend, and there were unspoken rules when it came to another male's female sibling. Rules which, at the moment, I wished didn't exist.

"Are you going to need my help?" Leah asked Mitch.

Yes. Now that I'd found her, the thought of being away from her, even if it was in a room down the hall, wasn't sitting well with my animal or me.

I tried not to read anything into Mitch's hesitation or the studious way he was watching Leah and me. "No, I think Bryson and I can handle it." He motioned for me to follow him.

"Okay, then." Leah rounded the counter and returned to the seat behind the desk.

No longer getting any attention, and without Leah's calming effect, the dog was back to whimpering. Not that I blamed him. Quills hurt a lot worse coming out than going in.

The exam area was a few steps down a short hallway. Other than some new landscape prints hanging on the walls, which I assumed were a result of Leah's influence, the room hadn't changed since I'd been here the last time. I made the mistake of glancing over my shoulder to get one more glimpse of Leah before entering the room and caught my shoulder on the doorframe. I jostled Bear, making him yelp, and gaining Mitch's scrutiny. Again.

"Sorry, boy," I muttered.

Mitch waited for me to pass through the doorway, then closed the door and circled to the other side of an exam table sitting in the middle of the room.

"You okay, Bryson?" Something in his tone made me think he wasn't asking about my shoulder. Had he figured out my connection to his sister?

No. "Fine." I was nowhere near being okay. I should be exhilarated that I'd found my mate, the one female on the entire planet who was supposed to be my perfect match. Instead, I wanted to punch something. Even though my parents and brother fell into the lucky category, I hadn't come close to having a decent relationship and, up until now, figured I was going to spend the rest of my life alone.

As far as good first impressions went, mine ranked on the lower end of terrible, with Leah thinking that I was linguistically challenged. To make matters worse, she was Mitch's sister, a human who had no idea that shifters existed. Even if her brother was willing to give me a free pass on the sibling-taboo rule, why would someone like her want to go out, let alone want to mate, someone like me? I was surly, a loner, and lacked the finesse or charm most women found appealing.

"Go ahead and set him here." Mitch patted the middle of the exam table.

He knew I wasn't a social creature and didn't try to engage me in conversation. If he had any questions about my behavior, he kept them to himself. An hour later, after a few growls and a couple of yelps, the quills were out. I spent another five minutes waiting for Bear to mark several trees on Mitch's property, then held a contemplative conversation with the dog in the cab of my truck before heading back to the lodge.

The entire drive was focused on Leah and the prospect, as uncomfortable as it was, of convincing her to give me a chance. Somewhere along the way, I'd reached the conclusion that I was in way over my head and needed help. The only person I could think of who came close to understanding what I was feeling was Nick. He knew all about having a human for a mate.

Mandy was the greatest. They'd gone through a lot, including her being kidnapped, before they finally got together. Of course, Nick had the advantage of his mate knowing all about shifters when he'd first started dating her.

Maybe Nick could give me some pointers on how to win over Leah. Help me figure out a way to tell her she was my mate, and that I could shift into a seventeen-hundred-pound bear without scaring the hell out of her.

LEAH

I stood near the window and watched Bryson back out of the driveway. As much as I avoided men, had sworn never to get involved in a relationship again, I couldn't help being drawn to him. It was the reason I was hiding behind the blinds and sneaking a glimpse of him through the window.

After walking Bear over to the trees and letting him do his business, Bryson had returned to his vehicle. He'd been sitting there for the last five minutes. I'd seen his lips move but couldn't tell if he was talking to himself or having a conversation with the dog.

He reminded me of an adorable teddy bear, a large, massively muscled, downright sexy teddy bear. I heard Mitch's sneakers squeak on the linoleum, let the blinds drop back into place, and scurried away from the window. The stack of magazines sitting on the table between the two guest chairs weren't out of place, but I pretended to straighten them anyway.

"See anything interesting out there?" Mitch asked as he used the counter to scribble something into a patient's file.

"Um, no, I mean…I was admiring the view."

"Are you talking about the landscape or Bryson?" Mitch, ever perceptive and annoying, teased, then closed the file and placed it next to the computer on my desk.

"The landscape, of course." I shuffled around him, hoping he didn't see the flush I felt burning my cheeks. I didn't need my brother chastising me about ogling one of his customers, even if there was a lot to appreciate.

"Right."

My thoughts had absently returned to Bryson and before I thought better of it, I asked, "Is he always like that?"

"Do you mean quiet, reserved, and straight to the point?" Mitch bobbed his head. "Yeah, pretty much. Why?"

"No reason." At least none I wanted to share. There were some topics a girl didn't discuss with her older brother. My fascination and attraction to a guy I'd just met was one of them.

Mitch glanced at the clock hanging on the wall in the

waiting area and said, "It's almost noon, so why don't you go ahead and call it a day."

"Are you sure?" I hated hearing the subtle desperation in my voice, the lingering self-doubt that still invaded my thoughts. Staying busy was my coping mechanism, and I'd hoped there'd be more work for me. The prospect of having nothing to do for the remainder of the weekend was unsettling.

"Positive. Why don't you get out, do something fun, go exploring?"

Unlike my mother, who didn't have a problem being pushy or overbearing, my brother used an encouraging approach. No matter whose advice I listened to, the message was still the same. They wanted me to stop hiding and start enjoying my life again. I self-consciously rubbed my arms. After what Caleb had put me through, I still wasn't sure if I was ready, or if it would ever be a possibility.

"You know the resort isn't that far from here. Maybe you should take a drive over to the lodge and have lunch. Berkley makes the best lasagna in the state." He slipped off his lab coat and hung it on a hook on the wall. "Or, you could hang out with me this afternoon. I need to drive over to Gabe's and take a look at one of his horses. Otherwise, I'd go with you."

"No, that's okay." The last time I'd gone with him to Gabe's, I'd ended up stepping in a pile of manure. No matter how many times I tossed my favorite pair of tennis shoes in the wash, I hadn't been able to get rid of the stains or the stench. I finally had to throw them away and buy a new pair. "Maybe I'll read a book or go for a walk."

"I'm not sure how long I'll be, so if you change your mind, don't forget to leave a note." He gave me one of his sympathetic looks. A look I'd seen more times than I'd wanted to during the short time I'd been staying with him. Mitch was great about supporting my independence, but after what happened, I didn't blame him for being concerned. Letting him know my whereabouts was a small price to pay for everything he'd done for me, for helping me when I needed it most.

"I will, and you have fun dodging horse poop." I giggled.

"Not to worry. My boots are in the truck." After giving me a quick hug, he headed for the door. "You know, if you go for lunch…" He paused with his hand on the door's metal bar, his lips slowly forming a mischievous grin. "You might get a chance to drool over Bryson some more."

I did not drool. I could hear Mitch's boisterous laughter coming from outside even after the magazine I'd thrown smacked the back of the door and dropped to the floor.

BRYSON

It was nearing the lunch hour when I pulled into the main entrance of the resort. Instead of heading back to the lodge, I took the side road leading to Nick and Mandy's cabin. Since I had to drop off Bear, I figured it was a good time to explain my dilemma to Nick and see if he'd be willing to help. Now that I'd found Leah, the longer I was away from her, the more agitated my animal got. He wanted his mate, and no amount of trying to reason with him would pacify his irritation.

My human side wasn't doing much better. There was a tightness in my chest, an unwanted tension rippling through my body and conflicting with my easy-going nature. I'd come close to turning around two or three times and heading back to Mitch's place. Not having a good enough excuse to explain my return or risking Leah thinking I was a stalker were the only things that stopped me.

"Let's get you inside." I scooped Bear off the seat and headed for the porch. Before my fist connected with the door's wooden surface, Mandy had it open and was reaching for the dog. "How's my poor baby doing?" She cuddled him close to her chest and nuzzled the fur at the base of his neck. The animal made pathetic whimpers, milking her attention for everything it was worth.

"Come on in." Mandy moved into the space between the living room and the small kitchen so I could enter. "Did Mitch have any problems removing the quills?"

"No." Though I was pretty sure the dog might disagree. "Mitch said he'd be fine." I dug into the pocket of my pants, pulled out the bottle of antibiotic tablets he'd given me, and set it on the half wall sectioning off the kitchen.

"Thank you." Mandy set Bear on the floor, then gave me a quick hug, her arms too short to circle my thick waist. "I really appreciate you taking care of him for us. Between dealing with the contractor and the wedding being less than two months away, I'm going nuts."

My mother always taught me to be respectful to females, no matter how trivial their needs. Any other time, I would hang around for a few minutes and listen to Mandy vent. I was anxious to resolve my dilemma about Leah and figured my mother would agree that this was one of those times when being abrupt could be overlooked. "Is Nick around?"

"Yeah." Mandy drew the word out, then narrowed her eyes suspiciously. "He's out back working on one of his projects. Why?"

Nick was quite the craftsman. In his spare time, he constructed furniture by hand and had even sold a few pieces to some of the locals. Once their new house was finished, he'd have a large shop where he could do his work. Until then, he used a small shed behind their cabin.

"No reason. Talk to you later." I escaped out the door before she could question me further. Rather than use the stairs, I jumped off the porch, shortening the distance to the shed. I peeked inside and found Nick manually sanding a large rectangular piece of wood. He'd worked up a sweat and had taken off his shirt, so the only clothes he wore was an old pair of worn jeans.

He hadn't bothered to put on a pair of shoes, which I suspected had something to do with his animal's nature. He was half wild wolf, a breed notorious for being antisocial with a tendency to go feral. Neither quality applied to Nick, not since he'd come to live at the resort and taken Mandy as his mate.

"Hey, Nick." I wedged through the narrow opening to get inside.

"What's up, Bryson?" Nick asked, then laid the sander down on the strip of wood. "Did Bear survive his visit with the doc?"

"He'll live." For the second time today, I struggled with what to say, how to tell him about Leah and ask him for help. I wanted our conversation to remain confidential and glanced toward the door, worried that Mandy might make a surprise appearance.

"Is there a problem? You seem a little nervous," Nick said.

Besides needing help, and lots of it, what do I have to be nervous about? "I was wondering if you could spare a few minutes to go somewhere and talk." My bear, dominant creature that he was, didn't see the problem, nor was he interested in getting assistance from another male. He was all about going back to Mitch's and claiming our mate. Simple.

"You mean somewhere where Mandy can't overhear us?" He grinned, then grabbed his T-shirt off the bench near the door.

"Yeah, if you don't mind." I blew out a relieved breath, glad I hadn't needed to say anything negative about his mate and risk pissing him off.

"Not a problem. I needed a reason to take a break anyway. And if I've smelled correctly, Berkley did some baking this morning." He leaned over and pulled on his shoes. "Let's take a ride up to the lodge and help ourselves to a snack while we chat."

"I could definitely eat." All the mate-related stress had given me an appetite. Berkley was the best cook around, and when it came to baking, she was even better than my mother. Not that I would ever say it out loud, risk hurting my mother's feelings, or give her a reason to box my ears.

CHAPTER TWO

LEAH

"I'm fine, Mom, really." It wasn't a complete lie. I didn't have nightmares anymore, the ones where I woke up in the middle of the night afraid some unwanted fiend who looked a lot like Caleb was in my room. I'd also stopped watching over my shoulder wherever I went and considered it making progress.

I tucked my cell phone underneath my chin and reached into the crisper drawer inside the refrigerator. I pulled out a tomato, a bag of chopped lettuce, and a package of sliced meat. After setting everything on the counter of the center island in the kitchen, I went back to holding the phone against my ear.

Dora Jacobson was a worrier, not that I blamed her. I'd given up my apartment, moved from California, and was living with my brother, all because Caleb, my ex-boyfriend, refused to accept that I'd broken it off with him and wouldn't quit stalking me.

"Is Mitch around? Maybe your brother can spare a moment out of his busy schedule to talk to me." It was hard to miss the exasperation in her voice. My brother had been evading her calls ever since I'd arrived. I assumed it had something to do with her pressuring him to find me dates. She was a firm believer that getting back in the saddle, on the bike, or mounting whatever you'd fallen off of would fix everything. She was also convinced that my life would be better if my brother hooked me up with one of his friends.

For Mitch, being supportive was one thing, playing matchmaker was another. Other than responding to my mother's calls with a text to let her know we were fine, he always managed to be out of the house during our scheduled weekly call.

"He had an emergency." I gave her the usual excuse, knowing I'd have no problem getting my brother to buy me a pint of double chocolate ice cream for covering for him again.

"He always has an emergency," she whined. "Don't the people there believe in bringing their pets in during office hours?"

"What can I tell you? We live in a wilderness area, and animals get hurt. It's not like they can schedule their problems." I inhaled a calming breath. "You know Mitch is the only vet on the mountain."

"I do, but it doesn't mean I wouldn't like to speak with my son once in a while. Find out how he's doing and whether or not there's a woman in his life."

My mother is obsessed. It was a good thing she couldn't see me shake my head and roll my eyes.

"Please tell him to call me as soon as he gets back."

"You know I will." I was happy to tell him whatever she wanted me to, but knowing my stubborn brother, it wouldn't matter.

"How's it going there? Do you still like working for Mitch?" My mother changing the subject meant temporary appeasement.

I knew she thought taking a job in my brother's office might cause problems between us. Instead, it was the opposite. Mitch had a laid-back attitude, made a good boss, and was surprisingly easy to live with. Being behind a desk and working with animals wasn't the same as dealing with a multitude of customers in a busy clothing boutique. It was, however, satisfying and a lot less stressful.

There were times when I missed my old life, missed my friends, missed the constant activity that came along with living in a city. Moving here had been a huge change, one that took some time to get used to. But the more time I spent getting to know Mitch's clients, the more I realized how much I enjoyed the interaction and being around animals.

"Things are good, and the job is going great." This call was the same as all the other late-Sunday-morning calls we'd had since I'd arrived in Ashbury. My mother and I had always been close. I knew she worried about me and hated me being so far away.

I wished things were different, that I could magically undo ever meeting Caleb, but I couldn't. And I'd learned from experience that dwelling on wishes wasn't going to change anything. I'd survived without a father, made it through my awkward teenage years without too many incidents and had convinced myself that I'd make it through this chapter in my life just fine.

At least it was the perception I clung to and was currently working to achieve.

Up until I'd met Caleb, I hadn't been doing too badly in relationships either. When I'd first met him, he'd been charming and fun to be around. After two months of dating, things gradually changed. He became possessive, even tried to manage the time I spent with my friends. After that came the unfounded jealousy where even a simple hello from another guy would set him off. It didn't take long for me to realize he wasn't someone I wanted to build a future with, and I ended the relationship. After a couple of weeks passed without hearing from him, I believed he'd moved on. At least I'd thought so until I started getting phone calls at all hours.

When I ignored Caleb's calls, he'd shown up where I worked, making a scene if I didn't talk to him. It had finally gotten so bad that I'd had to get a restraining order, not that it did any good. He still found a way to stalk me, to let me know he wasn't giving up on getting back together.

Thankfully, Mitch had come up with a solution, a way to take back my life. The job hadn't been part of the plan, more of an unexpected bonus. Natalie, his full-time assistant, had gotten married shortly after I arrived. She came to work a few days later and announced that she'd be quitting to stay at home and start a family.

"So." I could hear my mother tapping her nails on a hard surface. "Have you met any interesting men yet?"

And there it was, the question I dreaded answering every time she called. My experience with Caleb had disrupted my life, left me feeling vulnerable and afraid to take a chance on getting involved with anyone else. I knew my mother meant well, but I wished she'd give me a break and go back to bothering Mitch about finding a woman to settle down with.

"Yes, Mom. They are lined up around the corner and down the mountainside just to get a chance to take me out." I wasn't what you'd call glamorously attractive. I enjoyed eating and had a well-rounded figure. Most guys were interested in taller, leaner women, the ones who didn't eat sweets and survived on vegetables and salads. I would never be any of those things and didn't bother trying.

"No need to be sarcastic. You know I worry about you, especially after…"

After what happened with Caleb. I heard her choked sob and knew she was on the verge of crying. "I'm sorry, Mom. Everything is fine. I'm fine. You need to stop worrying." I pushed away the unpleasant thoughts of what Caleb had cost me and strolled over to the patio door.

Viewing the beautiful landscape of trees and wildflowers lining Mitch's property always had a calming effect.

"Sweetie, you know that not all men are like him, right? There are still some good ones out there," she said.

I instantly thought of Bryson and his flustered expression when he'd brought Bear into the office the day before. I smiled—not for the first time since meeting him—and wondered if he was one of the guys she mentioned. "I know," I said, hoping my mother was right.

Maybe it was time to stop living in fear, to start doing something different with my life, to stop wondering if every guy I met was going to turn out like Caleb. Maybe it was time to take Mitch's advice, to get out and do some sightseeing, or stop by the resort and have lunch at the lodge.

My brother had been protective of me since we were kids and wouldn't have recommended the trip if he didn't think it was safe. He also wouldn't have teased me about Bryson—an attraction I had yet to admit—if he had any reservations about the man's character.

I returned to the counter and stared at the contents I'd retrieved from the fridge. A sandwich for lunch didn't sound as appealing as a plate of lasagna. A plate of lasagna with the possibility of seeing Bryson.

LEAH

I glanced around the lobby in the resort's lodge and understood what Mitch meant when he'd said I'd enjoy the place's rustic charm. Next to the lobby was a gathering room for the guests. I could see portions of the mountainside through a bay window lining one wall. The remainder of the room was finished with a log cabin interior. Off to the right was a huge fireplace with a stone-covered mantel.

When my gaze landed on the long line of people

waiting to get into the restaurant, all the courage I'd gathered before making the drive faded. This was a bad idea. What had I been thinking coming here by myself? I should have waited for Mitch and made him come with me. At least then I wouldn't feel so alone and out of place.

The last time Mandy and Berkley had come by Mitch's office, they'd given me an open invitation to visit. I didn't want to interrupt them while they were working, so I didn't bother to ask the young woman behind the reservation desk to call them. I turned to leave, took three steps, then stopped when I heard a male voice calling my name.

After searching for the source, I spotted Bryson emerging from a hallway on the opposite side of the large room, and my stomach fluttered. His uniform was clean and well-pressed, a duplicate to the one I'd seen him wearing the day before. He clipped a radio on his thick leather belt as he ambled toward me. His shocked expression transformed into a hesitant smile. "What are you doing here?"

"It's my day off, so I thought I'd do some exploring."

Bryson was nervously glancing around, and I couldn't decide if he was glad to see me or wished I would leave. In case it was the latter, I rushed to give him an excuse. "I came here for lunch. Mitch mentioned something about Berkley being an awesome cook and that the restaurant was a great place to eat."

"Mitch was right. Did he bring you…or are you here with someone else?" He shifted back and forth on his feet, his voice straining when he asked the last part of the question.

"No, I came by myself." I didn't mention that it had taken me months to find the courage to venture out on my own or that there'd been a part of me hoping to run into him.

The tension in his broad shoulders slackened, and his pursed lips lifted into a grin. "That's good."

There was no way Bryson could know about my past, and I was a little confused why he thought me showing up alone was a good thing. At least he wasn't making an excuse to leave, though he wasn't saying anything either. He was obviously on duty, and I didn't want his standing around talking to me to cause problems with his boss.

I glanced back at the line, which hadn't gotten much shorter. "It looks like the place is pretty busy. Maybe I'll come back another time."

"I'd feel really bad if you'd made the trip all the way out here and didn't get to eat. I was on my lunch break, and if you don't mind eating in the employee's kitchen with me, I'll make sure you get fed."

Was it my imagination, or was he holding his breath waiting for my answer? "Are you sure it won't get you into trouble?"

"No." He shook his head and patted the radio at his side. "I'm the one they call when there are any suspicious characters hanging around. And since you don't look too suspicious, I'm sure it'll be fine."

I laughed. "Does that mean you think I'm only slightly suspicious?"

"I won't be able to answer that question without further investigation, which is why you'll have to come with me."

BRYSON

Hearing Leah laugh, and knowing I was the reason, eased the constricting knot I'd been carrying in my belly since I'd first seen her standing in the middle of the lobby alone. I couldn't believe she was here, couldn't believe she'd agreed to have lunch with me.

Though I'd overcome my inability to form words in her presence, I wasn't much of a conversationalist. I had no idea what I was going to say to her once I got her into the kitchen. I inhaled deeply and tried not to panic. I could do this—correction: I had to do this. Because now that I knew she was my mate, there was no way I'd walk away from her.

"Um, Bryson…" Leah bit the corner of her lower lip.

I'd been so focused on contemplating my next move that I hadn't realized there'd been a long pause in our conversation, and she was expectantly waiting for me to do something. I needed to do something, and quickly, before she had a chance to change her mind.

"Right… It's this way." I placed my hand in the middle of her back and urged her in the direction of the hallway leading to the kitchen.

Once inside, Leah took her time perusing the country-style kitchen with its stained wooden cabinets, center island, and large prep area. "This is really nice. You could fit half my old apartment in this place."

Mitch had mentioned having family in California, so I assumed that was where she'd lived previously. Though I couldn't figure out why someone with her gorgeous appearance would want to move to such a remote location. It was one of many questions I wanted to ask her, to know about her, but realized I'd have to take it slow. "When Reese, Berkley, and Nick inherited the place from their grandfather, they didn't have to do much renovating in here. Everything is in its original condition."

"Nick, as in Mandy's fiancé?" Leah stopped in front of the glass doors leading out to the patio, then glanced over her shoulder, her gaze mildly surprised.

"Yep, you could say it's a family business." In the year I'd worked at the resort, I'd grown attached to the siblings and their employees. They'd become my extended family, and I'd do anything for them.

I pulled a chair away from the table for her. "Have a seat, and I'll have our lunch delivered." I slipped the cell phone out of my pocket. I realized she had no way of knowing what was served in the restaurant, and hovered my thumb over the screen. "Sorry, I forgot to get menus. What would you like?"

"That's okay. I'm sure whatever you're having will be fine," she said, and smiled.

"Then I hope you like burgers and fries."

"That sounds great." I was pretty good at reading people, and seeing sincerity in her gaze over my food choice helped alleviate some of my stress. It was nice to know she wasn't being agreeable for the sake of politeness.

I placed a call to Nina, who was working at the registration desk. She must have seen me with Leah—the young female didn't miss much—because she didn't sound shocked when I added additional food to my regular order. After taking a seat across the table from Leah, I asked, "How do you like living in Ashbury?"

It hadn't occurred to me until I'd seen her without Mitch that there might be another male in her life, one she might be living with, one who was sharing her bed. The thought of another man caressing her lovely skin had my bear roaring with deadly intent since we'd left the lobby. It was the only question about her life that required an answer. The sooner the better.

Leah slipped the strap of her purse off her shoulder and hooked it on the back of the adjacent chair. "Oh, I don't live in town. I'm staying with Mitch."

Why was she living with her brother? Did that mean her stay here was temporary, that she would eventually be leaving? The loud, rapid beat of my heart drowned out my animal's rumbling. Before I could think of the best way to extract the information without her thinking I was being nosy, Paul, an employee who worked in the kitchen, scurried into the room.

He was carrying a tray containing two large platters filled with food, his attention focused on the floor. "Damn, Bryson, you hungry today or what?" His gaze landed on Leah, and the lanky, freckle-faced teenager came to an abrupt stop. "Oh, didn't know you had company. My bad." He set the tray on the end of the table between us and smiled at her. "Hi, I'm Paul. Let me know if you need anything else."

"I will, thanks." Leah stared with widened eyes at the plates containing two quarter-pound burgers and heaped with fries.

"Well, enjoy. We're having a crazy lunch hour, and I need to get back to the kitchen." Paul rushed out of the room at the same pace he'd entered it.

"Sorry, I forgot to tell Nina to bring you a single order." I pushed the tray aside after removing our lunch and the accompanying drinks, utensils, and condiments. "I'll eat whatever you don't want."

"Good thing, because if I tried to eat all this, you'd have to carry me to my car." Leah snatched a fry off her plate.

"I'd be more than happy to carry you wherever you want to go." Though her car was not the destination I had in mind. I much preferred my house, my bed, anywhere I could get her alone.

"Thanks, I'll keep it in mind." Leah's hand quivered as she took a bite.

At first, I was afraid my abrupt honesty might have scared her off. I was about to apologize until I noticed the sparkle in her gaze and the blush rising on her cheeks. Was it possible she might be considering the same thing? I could only hope.

We spent the next fifteen minutes devouring our lunch with a minimal amount of talking. I was pleased to see that Leah had a healthy appetite and didn't pick at her food like some of the females I knew who were always worried about maintaining their figures. As far as I was concerned, she was perfect with her ample curves in all the right places, enough to satisfy a big guy like me. Now all I had to do was convince her I was the right male for her.

"That was excellent." Leah pushed the plate in my direction. She'd eaten one of the burgers and half the fries.

"Are you sure you still have room for this?"

I nodded. "Yep, high metabolism." That and being part bear gave me a healthy appetite. I reached for the uneaten burger and had just taken a bite when I heard the stomp of boots in the outer corridor.

I caught the familiar scent of Seth, the newest member of our security team, seconds before he sauntered into the kitchen. "Hey, Bryson, are you having problems with your radio?"

"Turned it off. I'm on lunch."

"Preston has been trying to reach you."

"I'll call him when I'm done." Unless the place was on fire, and it wasn't, because I would have already smelled the smoke, there wasn't anything I could think of more important than spending time with Leah. Time that was quickly being ruined by Seth and his arrogantly charming grin. A grin I was seconds away from wiping off the damned wolf's face.

"Who's your friend?" He didn't wait for an answer before moving to Leah's side of the table. "I'm Seth. And you are?" he asked.

I was growling, my bear was growling, and Seth was going to suffer an insurmountable amount of pain if he got any closer to her.

"Leah," she said, then offered him a polite yet wary smile, which ensured he'd get to live, at least for today.

"Don't you need to get back to work?" I released a territorial rumble, a warning Seth couldn't possibly miss.

"Sorry, man. Didn't know." Seth took a few cowering steps backward. "I'll tell the boss you'll call him once you're done with lunch."

"Good idea." I grinned, watching Seth scramble to get out of the room.

"Is everything okay?" Leah asked. "You're not going to get into trouble for having lunch with me, are you?"

It pissed me off that Seth's interruption had caused Leah distress. "Not at all." I placed our empty dishes on the tray, then reached across the table to take her hand. "And even if I was, which I'm not, spending time with you was worth it."

CHAPTER THREE

BRYSON

Mandy snatched the plate of cookies off the counter and held them out of my reach. "Do you want to tell me what's going on? Why Nick and you have been acting so secretive for the last couple of days?"

Not really. "No idea what you're talking about." I had a thing for Berkley's chocolate chip cookies. They were freshly baked, and my mouth had been watering since I'd scented them and made a detour from Preston's office to snag some. I made another grab for the plate... And missed. Damn it, for a human, Mandy could move fast.

"Bryson." *Uh-oh.* I heard Berkley's voice behind me and cringed. It was the same you-are-in-the-worst-trouble-of-your-life tone she used with her brothers.

"Mornin', Berkley." I slowly turned to find her standing in the doorway with her arms crossed, her lips pressed into a determined line. "I was only going to take one, I swear." I'd seen Nick get his hand smacked a couple of times for snatching sweet stuff and hoped diverting the topic might work.

"Don't use that innocent tone with me." She strolled

into the kitchen, making sure to keep the doorway blocked so that I couldn't get around her. Not without picking her up and moving her aside, which she knew I'd never attempt. "I don't care about the cookies."

"Really?" I turned back to Mandy, held out my hand, and wiggled my fingers. She wrapped her arm protectively around the edge of the plate.

"I want to hear your answer to Mandy's question. And...I want to know if it has anything to do with the woman you had lunch with yesterday," Berkley said.

She was like the sister I never had, with the tenacity of an ornery terrier and a penchant for getting even by playing pranks on anyone who crossed her. Unlike her brothers, Reese and Nick, I'd been smart enough to stay off her radar. Until now.

When she wanted something, she didn't always play fair. To make matters worse, she'd have Mandy provide reinforcement. Unless the resort experienced a natural disaster in the next few minutes, there was no way I'd be leaving the kitchen without answering all their questions.

I puffed out an exasperated sigh and slumped my shoulders. "What do you want to know?" Sometimes, a guy, even a dominant bear who didn't take shit from anyone, knew when it was best to admit defeat, especially when it came to persistent females.

"For starters, we want to know about the woman Seth saw you with yesterday. Who is she?"

Damn that mangy wolf. I was going to inflict some pain the next time I saw him, which was going to be the minute I escaped from Mandy and Berkley's interrogation. Clawing might be too good for him. Maybe I'd have him moved to the night shift. A week patrolling the property when everyone was asleep might teach him to keep his observations to himself. I suppressed a grin, then said, "Her name is Leah."

"And?" Berkley tapped her arm one finger at a time.

"And what?" I stubbornly crossed my arms to mirror

her stance. "I answered your question."

"Where did you meet her?" Mandy asked.

I should have known I wasn't going to get off that easily. Mandy had been around Nick too long and had developed a keen method for dealing with a male's elusive stall tactics.

"I met her when I took Bear to the vet."

"Are you talking about Mitch's sister, that Leah?" Berkley asked.

"He might have mentioned it when I was there."

"Why were you having lunch together?" Mandy asked.

The steadily building pressure in my gut was getting worse. They knew something and weren't sharing. The smug, satisfied look that passed between them confirmed it.

I wanted to tell them it was none of their business, but didn't. Berkley had claws and knew how to use them, which meant certain parts of my male anatomy would be in jeopardy if I didn't give her a reasonable answer. "I ran into Leah on her way to the restaurant. Since she doesn't know anyone in the area yet, I offered to share my lunch with her." I thought the explanation sounded reasonable, straight to the point, no reason for them to be suspicious.

"That was thoughtful of you." Berkley smiled as if she thought I was a great guy. The darkening amber in her narrowed eyes, an influence from her wolf, meant she hadn't believed a word I'd said.

"You still haven't told me why you've been meeting secretly with Nick." Mandy taunted me by wiggling a cookie in front of my face.

Heat rose in my cheeks, and I was tempted to snatch it out of her hand with my teeth. These two were devious, treacherous, and could compete with any good law enforcement team on the planet. "He's helping me with some guy stuff."

"What kind of *guy stuff*?" Berkley asked.

"You know, stuff." I sucked at being vague and

wondered how the hell the other males did it so well.

Berkley uncrossed her arms and slid her hands to her hips. "This stuff wouldn't happen to have anything to do with the fact that Leah is your mate, would it?"

"What? How did you... Seth." I groaned and pinched the bridge of my nose. A week was too lenient for the male. I considered changing it to a month, along with some carefully placed paw swipes. Even though he'd heal fast, Seth might miss out on some of those sexual exploits he was always bragging about. It might not make him happy, but it would sure go a long way toward easing my frustration.

"It's because she's human, isn't it? And you weren't sure how to tell her." Mandy gave me a sympathetic smile, then handed me a cookie, which I stuffed in my mouth before she could change her mind.

"Forget about getting advice from my brother. He'll only screw it up," Berkley said.

Nick convinced Mandy to let him claim her, and they were getting married. How could anything he told me be wrong?

Berkley walked over to the table and pulled out a chair. "Have a seat."

"Why?" I asked.

"Because you want to know how to win over Leah, and we can help you." Berkley pointed at the chair. "Now sit."

Mandy set the plate of cookies on the table. Reluctantly, I did as she'd instructed. "I suppose it couldn't hurt to hear what you have to say."

CHAPTER FOUR

BRYSON

I'd been gripping the truck's steering wheel and staring at the door of Mitch's office for the last five minutes, trying to work up the nerve to go inside. As convinced as my animal was that we could win Leah simply by offering to claim her, my human half knew better. I'd never sought help from females in the past, and although Mandy's and Berkley's advice had been given out of friendship and caring, I still had reservations about their plan.

"This had better work," I told Bear, who was wedged between my thigh and a picnic basket on the front seat. He opened one curious eye and thumped my leg with his tail. There wasn't anything wrong with the dog. His muzzle was healing, and so far, he'd avoided another confrontation with one of the local porcupines. He was merely my excuse, not part of "the plan," so I could get in to speak with Mitch privately about Leah.

The vet was knowledgeable about shifters, did whatever he could to help our kind, and was aware that I was one. I'd witnessed how overprotective Reese and Nick could be when it came to their baby sister, so I figured the same could be said of most human males.

Although Mitch hadn't said anything the last time I was here, he was an intelligent man and seemed concerned about my behavior with his sister. I planned to be honest, to tell him she was my mate and hope he didn't run me out of his office with a shotgun. Or worse, make her leave town before I even got a chance to spend more time with her.

"I might as well get this over with." I couldn't believe I was talking to the dog again, a habit I'd gotten into a lot lately. I slid out of the vehicle and tucked him against my chest. I decided to leave the picnic basket in case I got turned down or needed to make a fast getaway.

Leah was sitting behind the reception desk and lifted her head as soon as I stepped inside. "Bryson," she said, giving me one of her bright smiles, the kind that made me think it was only for me. "I didn't know you had an appointment." She glanced at her screen, then at the dog. "Is everything okay with Bear?"

Time to work on the first part of my plan. "I don't have an appointment, but he's been scratching and acting a little bothered, so I thought it might be a good idea if Mitch took a look at him." The dog whimpered, adding to the guilt I already felt for bringing him to the one place that made him squirm.

"Do you have an opening? I can wait if he can't see us right away." I'd preferred dealing with Mitch first, but waiting meant spending more time with Leah, and neither my animal nor I had a problem with that.

"His next patient is running late. Let me see if he can get you in right now." She rose from her chair and disappeared around the corner.

Bear's whimpers escalated and included moaning. "It's for a good cause," I whispered, then scratched behind his ears. "I'll make it up to you later, I promise." If things went the way I hoped, I'd be more than happy to share some scraps from the picnic lunch Berkley had packed for me.

A few minutes later, Bear and I were in the exam room for the second time in a matter of days.

"I don't see any irritation." Mitch ran his gloved fingers over Bear's muzzle. "It appears to be healing fine." After removing the gloves and tossing them in the trash, he leaned against the counter opposite the exam table and braced his hands along the edge. "Bear's not the real reason you wanted to see me, is he?"

My plan, the only one I could come up with, hadn't seemed lame and transparent when I'd rehearsed it in my head. "I wanted to talk to you about…Leah."

"Are you having a problem with my sister?" Mitch pressed his lips into a thin line and straightened his shoulders.

Great, now he was on the defensive and thought I didn't like Leah. "No, no problem. It's…" I swallowed hard, having trouble saying the one word that could change our friendship.

"It's what?" He didn't sound overly upset, rather mildly amused, if the grin he was clearly trying hard to hide meant anything.

My skeptical and suspicious nature sprang to life. If I didn't know any better, I'd say he already knew why I was here. I couldn't tell if he approved, but it was apparent he wasn't going to make it easy for me.

"She's my mate." There, I'd said it. Not that it made me breathe any easier or lessened the stress pressing against my chest. Always one to be prepared, I placed a hand on Bear's flank, ready to snatch him off the table if Mitch told me to stay away from his sister and get the hell out of his office.

"That much is obvious." Mitch crossed his arms and quirked a brow. "What I want to know is what you plan to do about it. What are your intentions?"

My intentions. My intentions were the same as those of any full-grown male bear who'd been lucky enough to find his mate. I wanted to lure her into my bed, sink my cock into her sweet depths, and claim her. None of which I could tell her brother, so I gave him the sugarcoated version. "With your permission, I would like to start dating Leah."

"Leah's a grown woman and can make her own choices. But if it makes you feel better, you have my approval. And if, at some point, you get around to claiming her, you have my blessing for that as well." Mitch chuckled and lifted Bear off the exam table. "Why don't we get you checked out so you can take my sister on the picnic Berkley prepared for you."

"You know? She told you?" If my jaw was hanging any lower, I'd be stepping on it.

Mitch slapped a hand on the back of my shoulder. "Let's just say you've got some good friends who care a great deal about you and leave it at that."

LEAH

"This place is breathtaking." I smiled at Bryson over my shoulder, then continued scanning the secluded clearing, everything from the lush greenery covering the ground to the water cascading over a wall of boulders. What drew my attention most was the crystal-blue pond at the base of the rocks frothing with bubbles.

The Seneca Falls, one of the area's most visited tourist attractions, was more spectacular than I'd imagined. "How did you find this place?"

"One of the advantages of spending time in this area. You learn about all the secret places that aren't listed on the travel brochures," Bryson said as he unfolded a blanket and spread it on the ground.

Once Mitch had finished with Bear, a closed-door exam that lasted about ten minutes, Bryson spent a few more silent moments pacing across the reception area before asking me out on a picnic. He used the excuse of owing me a lunch because the one we'd had at the lodge was interrupted by his coworker. I didn't think it was necessary since I'd finished eating long before Seth had walked into the kitchen. Though I was a little hesitant about going on my first date since Caleb, a part of me had been excited by the prospect of spending more time with Bryson, so I hadn't argued the point.

I'd known him for only a couple of days but being with him was the safest I'd felt in a very long time. I was drawn to him in a way I'd never experienced with any other guy, and I didn't want to miss the opportunity to explore the connection further.

My brother, who'd disappeared during the event, magically reappeared and offered to take care of Bear. An offer that seemed too well timed not to be suspicious.

"Have you always lived in this area?" I sat on one corner of the blanket with my legs tucked to my side, then tugged on the hem of my skirt to keep it from hiking up my thigh.

"Born and raised." He grabbed two bottles of water out of an ice chest, then settled next to me, his large frame taking up a considerable amount of the blanket. After handing me one of the bottles, he snagged the large wicker basket containing our lunch and set it down in front of us.

I smiled at Bryson's brief explanation. In the short time I'd spent with him, I'd learned he was a man of few words and said only what he thought was necessary to make his point. I was a social creature, but I hated conversations filled with meaningless small talk. I appreciated his directness and how easy it was to talk to him.

Throughout our lunch at the lodge, the topic of a girlfriend had never come up. Bryson wasn't wearing a ring, so I didn't think he was married. He might not be considered overly charming, but he was a handsome guy with the most amazing dark brown eyes. His height neared six feet, and with the angled jaw, broad shoulders, and muscular physique, he probably had women throwing themselves at him regularly.

If he was in a relationship he'd forgotten to mention, I'd rather deal with the disappointing news now than hear about it later, after I'd allowed my emotions to get involved. Although, I feared it might already be too late for the emotional part. "Do you have family in the area?" I hoped the question didn't seem too obvious.

"Yep." He opened the basket and pulled out several white plastic containers sealed with matching lids and set them on the blanket. "My parents live over in Hanford, and my brother and his wife live in a suburb near Denver."

I clasped my hands in my lap. "Is that where you live? In Hanford?"

He stopped what he was doing and placed his hand over mine. I was mesmerized by the intelligence in his intense gaze. A gaze that seemed to push past my outer appearance and see the real me underneath. It was a little unnerving, yet reassuring at the same time.

"I own a house on a property in the woods not far from the resort. I live alone. I have no wife, no girlfriend, no kids, though someday I'd like to have a family."

I licked my lip, entranced by the refreshing honesty. He slipped his hand to my nape, drawing me closer, his lips covering mine. His kiss, though gentle, was filled with enough passion to ignite a fire in my core.

When he pulled away, his hand lingered on my cheek. "If there's anything you want to know about me, anything personal, all you have to do is ask."

"Okay," I answered through a breathless pant.

"Let's see what Berkley packed for us." He grinned and returned his attention to the basket, then continued to extract the contents, which included several more containers, some napkins and utensils. Once he had the covers removed, I noticed that Berkley had gone out of her way to prepare us a special lunch.

There were sandwiches made with freshly baked bread,

rotisserie chicken, and a variety of sliced vegetables. The potato salad had been made from scratch, and so were the peanut butter cookies.

"Does this mean you don't know how to cook?" I asked.

Bryson snorted. "I can prepare a meal when I have to, but when it comes to cooking, Berkley is the best. And since she volunteered, I wasn't going to tell her no."

After heaping food on two plates, he handed one to me, along with a napkin and fork. "I'll have you know I can grill meat better than most males in the area."

I thought it odd that he referred to other guys as males rather than men. He wasn't the first person I'd heard use the term and figured it must be part of the local culture.

"I'm sorry, your bragging rights only go so far. If you want me to believe you, then you'll have to prove it." I had no way of knowing if he'd wanted to see me again and couldn't believe I was daring him to spend more time with me.

I'd spent so much time hiding from Caleb, hiding from life, that being able to be myself and tease a guy I was interested in felt good. Really good.

"You're on. All I ask is that you bring an appetite."

CHAPTER FIVE

LEAH

I awoke with a mixture of anticipation and nervousness coursing through me. Tonight was my date with Bryson, the one where he promised to show me his home and cook for me. It had been almost a week since the day he'd taken me on a picnic and given me the first of many delicious kisses that left me wanting more.

Since then, we'd been on two more dates. The first was a candlelit dinner at the lodge. The second, a movie, followed up with ice cream at a cute little shop in Ashbury.

Then there were the two or three times I spoke with him every day. For a guy who didn't spend a lot of time socializing, Bryson had no problem conversing on the phone. More surprising were the I-can't-wait-to-see-you texts he sent, which included cute little bear emojis. Whenever Mitch walked into a room and I mouthed that I was on the phone with Bryson, he'd give me one of his stupid grins, then leave so I could have some privacy. His understanding and refusal to pry were the things I loved most about my brother.

Before I had a chance to crawl out of bed and get ready

for work, there was a knock on the door. "Morning," Mitch said, pushing the door open a crack and peeking inside. He'd already showered and was dressed in a pale blue cotton shirt and gray pants. "Since you've been putting in extra hours helping me with emergencies, why don't you take the day off?"

"But what about your regular patients? Won't you need my help with them?"

"It's the middle of the week, and I'm sure I can handle the three appointments on my schedule without you." He flashed a mischievous grin. "Besides, you're going to need all your strength for your big date tonight."

"It's only dinner." I couldn't believe my brother, the man who was notorious for threatening all my dates when I was in high school, was encouraging me to have sex with Bryson.

"If you say so." Mitch shrugged, then smiled. "Just in case it's not, I'll see you tomorrow."

I'd never been much of an athlete and was impressed when my pillow smacked him in the head before he could escape out the door.

His chuckle filtered into the room, along with his fading footsteps.

Staying in bed with the intention of getting a few more hours of sleep lasted for what seemed like five minutes. All I did was think about my brother's teasing words.

Would my date with Bryson lead to something more? And if it did, would I be ready? Thoughts of his delectable kisses and how safe I felt when he held me in his strong arms left me overheated, fighting with my pillow, and finally taking a lukewarm, nearly cold shower.

Doing menial chores around the house—my way of thanking my brother for letting me stay with him—wasn't much better and barely used up the morning. With time on my hands and energy to expend, I decided to do some hiking and explore the woods on Mitch's property.

Even though it was a sunny day and the weather was

pleasant, there were areas where the trees blocked out the dense rays and the temperature would be cooler. I knew better than to enter the forest unprepared. After scribbling a note to Mitch in case he came home early, I stuffed a light jacket, a bottle of water, and a couple of energy bars into a backpack I'd retrieved from his hall closet, then headed out.

Early spring on the mountain was alive with color. The new pink blooms on the shrubbery and the fresh scent of pine filtering through the air provided an aromatic enhancement to the scenic walk. As much as I enjoyed the beauty of my surroundings, my thoughts kept drifting to Bryson and our upcoming evening together. With his easygoing smile and attentive demeanor, the man was all kinds of enticing. Brawny, yet gentle.

The more time I spent with him, the more I felt like the old me. The me before Caleb and his stalking had upended my life. In a way, I had my bullying ex-boyfriend to thank for my current situation. If it wasn't for him, I wouldn't be living at Mitch's, and I never would have met Bryson. For the first time in a long time, I was finding new reasons to enjoy life again.

I'd been so caught up in daydreaming, I hadn't realized I'd lost track of time. I checked the clock on my cell phone and realized I'd been walking for the good part of an hour. I stopped to take a short break and down some water. After stretching the aching muscles in my calves, I turned around and headed back to Mitch's house.

I could've explored a little longer, but I wanted to make sure I had enough time to get ready for my date. Fewer meandering thoughts and more focus had me reaching the trees lining the edge of the driveway in no time. I had one foot on the gravel when I heard a familiar voice. A voice I'd hoped I'd never hear again. My heart raced. I shuddered and froze.

"Leah, open up. I know you're in there. I only want to talk." Caleb's voice drowned out the banging his heavy fist made on the front door. I didn't have time to worry about how he'd found me. My main concern was getting out of there before he saw me.

If Mitch had been home, facing Caleb wouldn't have been a problem. My brother would have kicked his ass, and after all the grief Caleb had put me through, I'd probably let him. But I was alone, and he was a muscular guy with a bad temper. He'd never actually hurt me, at least not physically, but his controlling behavior and unpredictability scared me. He'd gone to a lot of trouble to track me down, and I didn't believe he'd only come here to talk.

My car was the only one sitting in the driveway, which meant he'd parked his vehicle somewhere out of sight so I wouldn't see him coming. The house was too far away. Even if I did manage to get inside, I didn't think it would stop him from breaking a window to get to me.

My car keys were in my pocket. I quickly dismissed the idea of making a run for it. If he caught me before I could get inside and lock the doors, I didn't want to give him the chance to force me into leaving with him. My only alternative was returning to the forest and hoping he assumed I wasn't home and decided to leave. Of course, it meant he'd come back, but by then I'd have contacted my brother and involved the police.

It tore at my heart thinking about how Caleb's arrival would impact the future of my relationship with Bryson— the damage it would cause, the lack of trust. I should have told Bryson about my past, about the worst mistake I'd ever made. But I'd been afraid. Afraid of how he'd react, that he'd walk away. Now, everything I'd been afraid of was going to happen no matter how much I wished it wouldn't.

I needed to stop worrying about what might happen and focus on finding a safe place to hide. Someplace where I could stop, retrieve my cell phone from the bottom of my backpack, and call my brother.

Mitch's house was fairly isolated. His nearest neighbor was Gabe Miller. The elderly man rented out his horses and offered guided trail rides to the tourists. I knew how to find his place by car and was pretty sure which direction I needed to go by foot. If I headed toward Gabe's place, maybe I'd get lucky and run into one of his tours.

Cautiously, and as quietly as possible, I retreated backward into the forest. Unfortunately, I'd been so focused on the ground and watching where I was walking that I hadn't realized Caleb had moved to this side of the house and was glaring in my direction with angry brown eyes. "Leah, what are you doing out here, and why didn't you answer me?" He'd always been worried about his appearance, kept his hair styled and face clean-shaven. Now, stubble ran along his jaw. His cotton shirt was wrinkled, and his dark hair was longer, slightly mussed, as if he hadn't bothered to comb it in the last twenty-four hours.

Panicked, fear coursing through my veins, I froze. "Caleb you need to leave."

He took a menacing step forward, a crazed, determined gleam in his gaze. "I'm not leaving until you talk to me. Give me a chance to make things right between us again."

"There is no us. It's been over for months. Why can't you accept it and move on with your life?" I continued easing backward.

"There's someone else, isn't there?" He clenched his fists against his thighs. "That's why you moved here, isn't it?"

I curled my fingers into my palms. His words were familiar and reminded me of other arguments, other uncomfortable situations. Situations that always left me angry and trembling inside. Jealousy was one of Caleb's many issues, and admitting I was dating someone else would only make the situation worse.

"I'm staying with my brother because you wouldn't stop harassing me." Not much better as far as choices went, but I was tired of being afraid, tired of this asshole ruining my life. "Mitch will be home soon, so you need to leave before he gets back."

"You're lying. I called his office in Ashbury and found out that he's working until three. It's only two, and I plan to be long gone before he gets here." Caleb smirked. "And you're going with me."

No, I'm not. Caleb stomping toward me across the driveway was all the incentive I needed to turn and run into the forest.

"Damn it, Leah. Come back!"

BRYSON

"I've got it covered." No matter how much I wanted to growl, I wasn't going to let Berkley and Mandy know how exasperated I felt that they were still questioning me about my date plans with Leah. I knew they only wanted to help but this was the third time today they'd cornered me.

"Are you sure?" Mandy asked. "We want to make sure you have everything you need for tonight."

The ring from my cell cut through my groan. I slipped it from my pocket and saw Mitch's name appear on the screen and wondered why he'd be calling me. Instinctively, I knew it was about Leah. My pulse quickened, and I gripped the phone tighter. "Mitch, what's wrong? Is Leah okay?"

Concern flickered across Berkley's and Mandy's faces as they moved closer to overhear what Mitch had to say.

"I came home from work and found a note that she'd gone hiking. She should have been back by now. I searched near the house, but I can't find her." I could hear a long intake of breath before he continued. "I...I think something happened to her. I could really use your help."

"I'm on my way." I was already headed out of the employee kitchen and down the hallway, my pace frantic and increasing with each step.

Berkley, with her wolf's stealth, caught up with me as I reached the parking lot. "Bryson, what's going on?"

"Leah's missing. I need to…" It was all I could manage before yanking the truck door open and hopping inside.

Mandy had arrived seconds before and overheard what I'd said. "I'll find the guys." She spun around and rushed back toward the lobby.

By guys, I knew she meant Nick, Preston, and Reese. I was good at tracking, but Nick's wolf was better. If something bad had happened to Leah and I couldn't detect her scent, I'd need everyone's help to find her.

Please let her be all right. Let me find her in time.

"Don't worry, she's going to be okay." Berkley, always perceptive to others' emotions, figured out the direction of my thoughts. "Call me on the radio as soon as you know anything. Now go. We'll be right behind you." She stepped away from the truck and closed the door.

I stomped on the gas pedal, not caring that I sprayed the lot with gravel. Getting to Leah was all I could think about.

Fortunately, the traffic between the resort and Mitch's house was light. Otherwise, the twenty-minute drive I'd condensed to ten by taking the curves in the road at an accelerated rate might have ended in a head-on collision. My bear roared and bared his teeth the entire way. He didn't care about safety either, not when our mate was in trouble.

Mitch reached my truck seconds after I skidded to a stop in his driveway. "Leah's a careful hiker, and she wouldn't have gone far." He scrubbed his hand through his hair, his gaze briefly glassing over. "I don't know what could've happened to her."

"Give me a second." I moved away from Mitch, sniffing the air until I caught a hint of lavender body wash Leah used and followed it. When I reached the tree line, I found an area where the scent was a little stronger. What I hadn't expected to find was the odor of an unfamiliar male. Jealousy rode me hard. "Was Leah seeing someone else?" I reacted before thinking and snapped at Mitch, the gravelly growl of my bear leaking into my voice.

Mitch was walking toward me and stopped. He knew enough about shifters to recognize when our animals pushed for dominance. He shuffled a few steps backward, keeping his gaze focused on the ground. "No... No way. She was looking forward to your date."

Mitch was right. Why would Leah be seeing someone else or invite them to her brother's place after we'd made plans? She was a good person, would never do anything to hurt me or anyone else. If I wanted to find her, I needed to stop reacting emotionally and start thinking logically.

Something about this whole situation wasn't right. I pinched the bridge of my nose, trying to calm my bear and regain control of my emotions. "Sorry."

"Bryson, what's going on? Why would you even ask me something like that?"

"Because I can smell another male, a human. The scent intermingles with hers." I drew air through my mouth, lessening the other male's odor in order to soothe my agitated animal.

Confused, Mitch scratched his jaw. "Are you sure?" he mumbled, then noticed my frown at the rhetorical question and said, "Of course you are."

"Any idea who it might be? Could a patient have stopped by, someone with an emergency?" I hadn't detected any recent animal odors and knew I was grasping for possibilities.

"No. They all know I work in town during the week. If someone had shown up, Leah would have called me." Mitch shook his head. "It doesn't make any sense. Unless those calls..." His cheeks paled.

"What calls?"

"Leah mentioned getting hang-up calls a couple of days in a row. I thought it was a little strange at the time but dismissed it. Now I'm wondering if it was Caleb, if he somehow found out she was staying here."

"You're not making any sense. Who is Caleb and what's his connection to Leah?" *And why didn't she mention him to me?*

"He's a guy she was dating about a year ago." Mitch's troubled gaze held mine. "A real piece of work with a bad temper. He started stalking her after she broke it off. It's the reason she was staying with me."

Hearing that Caleb had tormented my mate, might still be tormenting her, made me want to tear him apart. Holding back my bear's overwhelming need to shift was growing steadily harder. I clenched my fists to keep my claws from easing out of my fingertips.

"Since Leah's car is still here, do you think he…" Mitch asked.

I blocked out the images of Leah being forced into a vehicle and carted off against her will. I refused to believe she was gone and clung to the hope that she was somewhere close by. I briefly closed my eyes, freeing my mind of troubling thoughts and allowing the extensive training Preston required every member of the security team to take. One of the first things I'd learned was not to dismiss anything out of the ordinary. No matter how small or inconsequential my observation might be, it was important.

Then I remembered seeing a car parked on the side of the road near the turnoff to Mitch's property. At the time, I'd been so focused on getting here that I hadn't given it much thought. The red car had California plates. It was too much of a coincidence to think the vehicle didn't belong to the male I'd scented. "There's a car parked on the main road not far from here. Any idea who it belongs to?"

"I saw it too and thought it was tourists," Mitch said. "People stop on occasion to take pictures."

"If you're right about the male being Caleb, he might

have parked there so Leah wouldn't see him," I said.

Mitch smacked himself in the head and dug his phone out of his back pocket. "I'm such an idiot. Because cell service is intermittent in this area, after she moved here, I upgraded her phone to include GPS tracking without getting a signal."

After a couple of taps on the screen, Mitch held the device up so I could see it. "Unless she doesn't have her phone with her, according to the map, she's halfway between Gabe's place and here."

Seeing the red dot in the middle of the screen gave me a minimal amount of relief. It confirmed that she was nearby, but it didn't tell me if Caleb was with her or if he'd done something to hurt her. If the male had touched Leah in any way, getting back to his vehicle safely would be the least of his problems.

"When the others get here, tell them everything you told me. Then have Nick scent the car to confirm whether or not it belongs to the same male." I knew Mitch would want to help search for Leah, but I didn't want him coming with me. There was no guarantee I'd be able to control my bear if anything had happened to her. My animal going feral wasn't something Mitch needed to see.

The sun was setting and it would be dark soon, which meant the temperature would drop, and quickly. Leah was human, didn't possess the additional body warmth an animal form supplied, and would freeze. The only way to save time and get to her faster was if I transformed into my bear. I toed off my boots, then ripped opened my shirt, sending buttons flying through the air. Clothes could be replaced. Leah couldn't.

CHAPTER SIX

LEAH

It was a good thing I'd paid attention to landmarks every time I'd ventured out into the woods close to Mitch's house. I'd gotten familiar with some of the narrow paths, varied tree clusters, and the occasional rock formation. It was one of the advantages I had to get away from Caleb. He was a city boy who hated the wilderness, always had an excuse whenever I'd invited him for walks in the park near my old apartment.

With any luck, I'd be able to use the natural surroundings to elude him. Maybe he'd get frustrated and give up chasing me. I tried not to let the fact that he'd tracked me all the way to Colorado discourage me from clinging to the glimmer of hope.

Running was never something I'd enjoyed, had actually learned to hate it from the first day my high school instructor made our class do laps in gym class. At the moment, it was the only thing I could do to put some distance between us.

When I reached a point where my ribs ached, my lungs burned, and I didn't think I'd be able to make it another step, I glanced around, searching for somewhere to hide. Off to my right was a downed tree trunk balancing diagonally across a mound of rocks. It wasn't ideal, and I wasn't exactly skinny.

My hair caught on the bark, painfully pulling out several strands as I wedged into the compact space. The ground, covered with decaying leaves, was cold, damp, and seeped through my jeans. My knees were jammed tightly against my chest, and the jagged edge of the boulder pressed uncomfortably against my back.

Caleb was close. I couldn't see him but I could hear him stomping through the underbrush. He repeatedly yelled my name, which turned into ranting, then finally cursing. The rapid pulse beating in my chest and thrumming in my ears was so loud, I was afraid he'd hear it.

I clamped my hand over my mouth and forced myself to take small, shallow breaths. Long after Caleb's voice began to fade, I remained hidden with my backside going numb and my calf muscles cramping.

I'd seen too many scary movies where one of the characters had been fooled into believing they were safe and made the mistake of leaving their hiding place too soon. I remained hidden, an uncomfortable pretzel with my knees pressed tightly to my chest. I was going to be the heroine, the one who survived and got the handsome hero at the end of the show.

Thinking about heroes reminded me of Bryson and the possibility of losing him. I swiped at the moisture building in my eyes, then pushed the thought from my mind. Dwelling on what-ifs wasn't going to help with my current situation.

It took some maneuvering, but I was able to find and remove my cell phone from my pack. I swiped the screen to call my brother and let him know I was in trouble, then resisted the urge to scream when I saw the "no service available" icon.

Other than the occasional squawk or flutter of bird wings, the surrounding area had been quiet for some time. My resolve to remain in the cramped hole beneath the decaying tree trunk lasted for as long as it took my bladder to rebel. I dusted the dirt and dead leaves off my pants while I waited for the tingling in my legs and backside to subside. I found a place near a tree where I could relieve myself without anyone sneaking up on me.

With the dwindling sunlight came cooler temperatures, and I was glad I'd had the foresight to tuck a jacket into my backpack. I still wasn't certain Caleb had stopped searching for me. I didn't want to risk running into him if I headed back to Mitch's house, so I opted for making my way to Gabe's place instead. The people who lived on the mountain looked after each other. At Gabe's, I wouldn't be alone, and he'd have a phone I could use to call my brother.

It didn't take long for my fantasies of warmth and security to diminish. I'd walked a short distance and realized that nothing looked familiar. Somehow I'd gotten turned around and wasn't sure I was headed in the right direction. On top of being lost, I thought I heard twigs snapping. Glancing behind me without stopping cost me. I didn't see the partial tree root running above the ground.

I caught the tip of my boot on the exposed edge, tripped, and stumbled forward. All the flailing and attempting to right myself didn't stop me from losing my balance and hitting the ground.

The jolt to my knees was nothing compared to the sharp pain that shot through my ankle when I tried to stand. I winced, my hiss expelled through gritted teeth. To make things worse, I'd scraped my hands when I'd braced against the fall. Though most of the cuts were superficial, I'd managed to slice the flesh on my left hand bad enough for blood to run between my fingers and stain the edge on the sleeve of my jacket.

Not good, not good, not good. I trembled. Didn't blood

49

attract wild animals? Like wolves…and bears. A rabbit was the largest creature I'd seen during my hikes, but I'd never been this far from the house either. I tried to remember the things I'd learned on the camping trips my family had taken when I was a child. Though I loved nature and enjoyed being outdoors, Mitch was the expert when it came to trekking through the wilderness.

I gulped in air and pushed past the panic keeping me immobile. I scanned the area searching for a suitable place where I could get the weight off my foot and address my wounds. After finding a nearby tree where the ground was free from shrubbery and smoothed out enough for me to sit semi-comfortably, I hobbled toward it, then used the trunk as an anchor to lower myself to the ground.

The fear I had of Caleb was nothing compared to the fear I had of attracting a four-legged predator. Using my injured hand, I pulled the backpack into my lap. I retrieved the bottle of water, balanced it against my thigh on the ground next to me, then checked the additional zippered pockets for anything I could use to wrap my hand.

I could have kissed my brother when I found a pocketknife. It wouldn't provide much protection if I got attacked, but it worked great at cutting a strip of fabric from the bottom of my T-shirt.

I took a small sip of the water, then leaned to the side and poured what was left over the bloody cut. Once I wrapped and secured the material around my hand, I rolled up my pant leg and braved a glimpse at my ankle. The area above my boot had swelled with a hint of bruising. I didn't think it was broken, although with a sprain, there was no way I could walk to Gabe's or anywhere else, not without a lot of help.

Hopefully, Mitch hadn't been called out on an emergency, would arrive home at his usual time, and find my note. If not, I was in for a long cold night without anyone besides Caleb knowing what had happened to me.

My thoughts turned to Bryson. What would he think

when he showed up for our date and I wasn't home? Would he try to call me and assume I didn't want anything more to do with him when I didn't answer?

I'd finally met a great guy. One I cared about, one who'd stolen my heart, and one I hoped I might have a future with. Now, thanks to Caleb, I might never get the chance. The idea of losing Bryson weighed heavily on my thoughts, more painful than any of my physical injuries, more upsetting than the prospect of becoming an animal's dinner.

The emotions I'd worked so hard to control since Caleb's arrival burst from their restraints. The overwhelming gush of despair was more than I could stand, and when the tears rolled down my cheeks, I let them.

BRYSON

I didn't give Mitch a chance to argue. I let the shift wash over me—bones snapping, limbs changing, fur sprouting. I entered the forest with anxiety pulsing along every nerve of my transformed body.

Caleb's scent was closely interwoven with Leah's, making it hard to keep my animal from destroying everything in his path. Even if Leah had somehow managed to escape the male, she was out there alone. She could be lost, hurt or…worse. I refused to consider the latter.

I pushed myself harder, digging my paws into the hardened ground, bounding between trees, ignoring paths and barreling through underbrush. Though I headed in the general direction I'd seen on Mitch's GPS, I continued to follow Leah's scent. Technology was useful, but what if something happened and she'd lost her phone? I wasn't willing to take the chance and risk wasting time getting to her.

There were areas where dead leaves, dampened by recent rainfall, made it hard to retain her scent. I growled my frustration every time I had to stop, retrace my steps and sniff the ground until I caught another trace of Leah.

Eventually, Caleb's irritating odor ventured off in a different direction from hers. The urge to chase after the male and tear him to shreds was strong, but the need to find my mate was stronger. Not long afterward, her trail led me to a downed tree braced at an angle against some boulders. It was obvious by the strength of her scent coating the area underneath that she'd spent some time hiding in the narrow space. How long or how recent was harder to determine.

At first I'd assumed she was headed to Gabe's place, but the longer I searched for her, the more concerned I became that none of her tracks were headed in any specific direction. It didn't take long for her scent to grow stronger or for me to increase my pace. A few minutes later, I entered a clearing and saw her on the ground, huddled against the trunk of a wide tree.

She's alive. Relief swept through me. The unyielding tightness in my chest eased until I detected a faint scent of blood. Other than the hand she'd wrapped with fabric from her T-shirt, I didn't see any obvious injuries. If she'd gotten lost, as I suspected, why hadn't she tried to find some shelter rather than enduring the cold by being exposed?

"Crap." Leah pursed her lips, her narrowed gaze focused on tearing open the cellophane wrapper of an energy bar with shivering fingers. In the short time I'd known her, I'd never heard her cuss. It wasn't an appropriate time to be amused, but I couldn't help it. The cute way she wrinkled her nose was adorable, and if my bear could have formed a grin, he would have.

It didn't take long for her to realize I was there. I cringed when she slapped a hand over her mouth to stifle a scream. I'd been too concerned about finding her when I'd shifted that I hadn't even considered how she'd react the first time she saw my bear without knowing it was me. I wanted to rush over to her, to wrap my paws around her, share the warmth from my fur and reassure her that she was safe. Instead, I remained stationary, not wanting to scare her or make the situation worse.

"Nice bear. Please don't eat me." With shaking hands, she tossed the bar so it landed on the ground in front of me. "I know it's not much, but I'd appreciate it if you didn't make a meal out of me."

This was the moment I'd been dreading. I needed to transform and hope it didn't send her screaming and running through the forest. It would kill me to see fear or disgust in her expressive eyes, but it was a risk I had to take. Whether or not she allowed me to remain in her life after I revealed my true nature was moot. Her welfare and safety were my primary concerns.

And once I saw to her needs, I'd hunt down the male who'd put her life in jeopardy and ensure he never came near her again. On the topic of ridding Caleb from Leah's life forever, my bear and I agreed.

CHAPTER SEVEN

LEAH

A bear.

Could my day get any worse? First Caleb, then a sprained ankle, and now a grizzly bear the size of a flipping horse was standing on all fours not more than fifteen feet away from me. The cold had seeped through my clothes to my skin, shivers racked me, my teeth chattered. My backside was numb again from sitting in one place too long, and my hands shook so badly, I struggled to tear the cellophane wrapper off my last energy bar.

I hadn't heard the animal approach, only sensed its presence. I was going to be torn to shreds, going to die in the middle of nowhere without getting the chance to see Bryson one last time, to tell him how I felt.

I'd hoped by tossing the energy bar in his direction that the animal would take pity on me, snatch the snack, and walk away. No such luck. He ignored my offered treat and continued staring at me with an unnerving intensity. He didn't rise up on his haunches, bare his teeth, or growl. All the behaviors I'd have expected from a bear who'd found a tasty morsel in his territory. I knew it was weird and bordered on impossible, but it appeared as if he was contemplating the situation and the best way to handle it.

Then he grunted, the tone so similar to Bryson's I was certain I'd imagined it. Maybe I'd been sitting here freezing so long my brain cells had gone numb. I was even more convinced I'd taken the road to delusional when I heard the sound of bones snapping and, minutes later, saw Bryson standing naked in the exact same spot where I'd seen the bear.

No matter how many times I blinked or rubbed my eyes, it didn't change the fact that he was there and the bear wasn't. He presented a fine specimen, all hard, sculpted muscle. Under different circumstances, when I wasn't worried about my sanity, I'd be scrutinizing, drooling, and appreciating the view.

"Bryson." My voice rasped from a dry throat. "Where did the bear…" My delayed reaction to what I'd just witnessed slammed into me with enough force to knock me off my feet if I'd been standing. The animal hadn't gone anywhere. Bryson *was* the bear. Once my mind caught up with reality, everything I knew about him made sense. His large size, the growling, the overly protective behavior…

"I'm the bear, but please don't be afraid." He held out his hands. "I'm not going to hurt you."

"I'm not afraid." Confused, surprised, and maybe a little pissed that he hadn't told me before now, but I wasn't scared, not really. That I was safe in his presence was the one thing I could honestly say I knew for certain.

"You're not?" He widened his eyes and took a few hesitant steps toward me. "Me being able to transform into a bear doesn't surprise you." It was more a confused statement than a question.

"It would if I didn't already know shifters existed." It tore at my heart to see his pained expression. Was he afraid I would reject him because of his animal side?

I had a lot of questions, most of them revolving around

the future of our relationship, but I wasn't the type of person who ignored someone because they were different. If I could have run across the clearing and thrown myself into his arms to reassure him, I would have.

"How did you find out... Who told you?" He sounded relieved and curious at the same time.

"If you promise not to make me the main course in your next meal..." I teased with a nervous smile, then held out my hand.

"No promises," he said, taking a seat in the dirt next to me.

Part bear or not, having him this close sent flutters dancing around in my belly and heat coursing through me. It reminded me he was sitting on the ground with nothing protecting his backside. Thinking about his shapely ass reminded me he was naked, which had me staring at his lap, or rather at his cock, which was twitching to life. I was freezing, but it warmed me to know even under such awful circumstances, I affected him. And greatly, judging by the size of his growing erection.

I had to remind myself that now was not the time to be ogling the man, and forced my desirous thoughts, along with my gaze, back to his face. Flustered by his amused grin, I focused on his question.

"I went along with Mitch on an emergency call to one of the nearby properties to assist with a horse. I learned about shifters the hard way when the couple's youngest son transformed into a wolf cub in my lap." A vivid memory that required quite a bit of explaining by my brother and two shots or more of whiskey.

"That would do it." His easy laugh drew me in, and I relaxed.

My thoughts returned to the state of his body in the current elements, and I worried about his lack of clothing. "Aren't you cold? Would you like to use my jacket... You know, to..." As big as he was, the material wouldn't cover much.

"I'm part bear, remember? I can tolerate the cold for an extended period of time." He placed his hand over mine to keep me from slipping the sleeve from my arm.

"Okay." Good information to have. "How did you know where to look for me?"

"Mitch found your note, got worried when he couldn't find you, and called," Bryson said.

I read somewhere that animals tracked by scent. Was that how he'd found me? And if so, had he been able to smell Caleb as well? I wanted to ask but needed to explain about my past first, then hope he didn't dump me at my brother's place with an it-was-nice-knowing-you goodbye. "Aren't you going to ask me what happened? How I ended up out here?"

"We can talk about it later. Right now, I want to take care of you, get you somewhere safe and warm."

"I'm afraid we have a problem." I pulled on the hem of my pants, exposing my swelled ankle. He swept his fingertips lightly across my skin and growled. Why was he growling? I braced myself for a lecture on the dangers of not paying attention when hiking.

Instead, he pulled my pant leg down, then got to his feet and held out his hand. "Let's go."

"Go where? I can't walk, and unless your truck is parked nearby…"

"I left everything at Mitch's place," he stated in a calm matter-of-fact tone.

"How do you suggest we get back?" I slipped the backpack over my shoulder, then allowed him to help me off the ground. He kept his arm around my waist until I'd steadied myself on my good leg.

"I'll carry you." He grinned, as if traipsing through the forest naked and carrying me back to my brother's house wasn't a big deal.

"That's a long way to go, and I'm not exactly light." I smacked the rounded curve of my hip.

"It will be faster if I change into my bear and have you

ride on my back." Concern etched his brow. "Unless it makes you uncomfortable."

Finding out that he could turn into a bear didn't bother me nearly as much as seeing the doubt and worry in his eyes. "I'm fine with it if you are."

"Good. Can you stand on your own?"

"I think I can manage." I removed my hand from his arm and pressed it against the tree trunk for support.

He put some distance between us. The air filled with snaps and crackles and the bare, muscled butt cheeks I'd been staring at shifted shape and were covered with a thick dark brown fur. Bryson's bear was bigger than I remembered, and I had to admit I was a little intimidated when he lumbered toward me.

I knew Bryson wouldn't hurt me but I wasn't sure about his animal. I hoped Mitch hadn't been lying when he'd told me that a shifter's human side remained in control unless their animal turned feral.

He wasn't growling or acting like he wanted to attack me, so I cautiously held out my hand. He slipped his head under my palm as if he were an overgrown dog and encouraged me to scratch him. "Such a nice bear," I cooed, then giggled when he pressed his nose against my abdomen and snorted.

When he pulled away and turned to the side, I assumed playtime was over and he was ready to leave. There was no easy way for me to climb on his back. The ridge along his spine was too high off the ground for me to reach. "I don't suppose you know where we can get a stepping stool?"

With a shake of his head and what I interpreted to be a low chastising rumble, he pressed his belly to the ground.

"No need to get snippy. I was just asking." I grabbed a handful of fur, hoisted myself up, then stretched my leg over his thick girth until I was straddling his back. Once I was situated, he rose on all fours and headed in a different direction from when he'd arrived. "Wait, where are you going? Isn't Mitch's place back the other way?"

His bear's huff was a typical Bryson response, letting me know that he was going to do whatever he wanted.

I puffed out an exasperated breath. "Fine. Have it your way." I knew arguing was pointless and decided to make myself comfortable by pressing my chest along the ridge of his back and sinking my hands into the soft, warm underlayers of fur next to his skin.

BRYSON

It had been hell taking things slow with Leah once I'd found her. When I'd seen the fabric wrapped around her hand, all I wanted to do was pull her into my lap and touch every inch of her body to ensure she wasn't hurt anywhere else. I also had questions about Caleb, wanted the answers from her. After what Mitch told me, I knew pushing Leah was the wrong thing to do. I'd have to wait until she was ready to tell me.

In the meantime, I wanted her out of the forest and safe. I was overjoyed when she accepted my proposal and climbed onto my bear's back. It was an unexpected bonus, one I planned to utilize to my advantage. I ignored her when she tugged the fur on my neck, trying to get me to turn around and head toward Mitch's house. Since I was in animal form, I couldn't tell her I was taking her to my place. Not that I would have mentioned it in my human form either.

This wasn't the date I'd envisioned with Leah, but it didn't mean I wasn't going to move forward with my plan. I still needed to tell her she was my mate. Hopefully, with the shifter hurdle out of the way, telling her how much I cared about her and that I wanted to claim her would go a lot smoother. Although it had only been a couple of weeks, it hadn't taken more than our first kiss for her to win over my heart.

When I was younger, my father told me that once the bond was recognized, the emotional part for our human side followed considerably more quickly than it did for non-shifters. A human's love-at-first-sight scenario didn't always last a lifetime. Not so for our kind. Once we found our mate, we claimed and formed a permanent bond. A bond that nothing and no one could ever break. Now that I had Leah to myself, I'd take care of her in every way possible and prove to her that I'd make a good partner.

I still needed to let Mitch and the others know she was safe, and planned to make it my second priority as soon as we reached my house. I'd also inform them that she'd be staying with me for the evening, preferably in my bed, though I'd be sure to omit that particular detail during our conversation.

As much as I wanted to strip her naked and explore every inch of her glorious body, I was more concerned about her injury and wanted nothing more than to hold her in my arms all night if she'd let me.

Even with my steady pace, the trip took a little longer than expected. I'd skirted certain areas to avoid traveling over uneven ground and jostling Leah's injured ankle. My bear had no complaints. He was content to have her chest pressed against his back, her hands buried skin-deep in his fur.

As soon as we arrived at my place, I padded up the porch, the movement activating an automatic sensor and covering us with light. I dropped to my belly and waited for Leah to slide off my back. Once she had a solid grip on the railing and the pressure off her foot, I returned to the ground below and let the shift wash through me.

"Where are we?" Leah hopped so she could get a better view of the front of the house.

"This is my place." I refrained from saying "our home" as I joined her on the porch again. It was too soon to share that particular intention with her. I needed to make sure she accepted me as her mate and was comfortable with my animal side before talking about a future together.

I reached for the handle on the front door and pushed it open. I lived in a secluded area and never had any uninvited visitors, so I'd never worried about locking the doors. That would change with Leah being here.

Without giving her a chance to object, I scooped her into my arms.

"Bryson, what the heck?" She squealed and wrapped her arms around my neck.

"I told you I was going to take care of you." I chuckled, then elbowed the door the remainder of the way open and carried her inside. My work schedule kept me busy, and I wasn't always the neatest of people. I was glad I'd spent the previous evening cleaning and preparing for our date.

After tapping the light switch, I headed into a large open room with the living room on one side and the kitchen on the other. Ceiling-high bookshelves, along with a set of drawn blinds that concealed sliding glass doors leading out onto a deck where I'd planned to barbecue our supper, adorned one wall. I stepped between a rectangular coffee table and a plush tan sofa, gently setting her sideways with her legs extended across the soft cushions, then perched on the table beside her. All my furniture was built to accommodate my large size, and her smaller frame barely covered one end.

Leah looked around the room, her gaze stopping first on the stone fireplace, then smiled with appreciation at the center island and custom-crafted dark wood cabinets in the kitchen. "You're place is impressive," she said, returning her attention to me. My heart filled with pride at the admiration reflected in her gaze.

"Thanks," I said, then cupped her nape and tenderly covered her mouth with mine. She moaned against my lips, and I couldn't help drawing out the kiss until we were both breathless.

"I should call Mitch," Leah said after I released her. "He's probably going crazy wondering what happened to me." She reached for the backpack dangling by its strap on her arm. She set it on her lap, then dug through the contents until she pulled out her cell. "Err, the battery's dead."

"I'll take care of it. I promised Berkley I'd check in once I found you." Since I'd left my cell at Mitch's place, along with my truck and clothes, I reached for the cordless phone sitting next to a lamp on a nearby end table. Most of the time, I used my cell. But every now and then, reception in the area was bad. I kept a landline more to appease my mother's nagging than I did for emergencies. After hitting the autodial for Berkley's cell, I waited for her to answer.

"Bryson, did you find her?" she asked after one ring.

"Yeah, tell Mitch she's fine and I'll bring her home tomorrow." I hadn't thought to ask Leah if staying overnight would be a problem and expected her to protest. She raised an inquiring brow but didn't say anything. My bear rumbled his approval. Neither one of us wanted her to leave now that we finally had her in our home.

"Can you have someone drop off my truck in the morning?"

"Nick will take care of it. Mitch said to tell you he was right about the guy being Caleb." Now was not the time to ask what Nick had done to the male, not with Leah listening intently to my side of the conversation. Berkley didn't sound concerned, so I assumed her brother hadn't lost control of his wolf and damaged Caleb in any way.

"Thanks," I said.

"Sure. Do you need anything else?"

I wasn't in the mood to answer questions or receive any more unsolicited dating advice. I wanted to take care of Leah. "No," I said, disconnecting the call.

"Everything okay?" Leah shuddered and rubbed her arms.

Since I didn't have a fire going in the fireplace and kept the heat on a low setting during the day, the temperature inside the house wasn't much higher than it was outside. "Fine," I grumbled, irritated with myself for not taking care of her first. I grabbed the blanket draped across the back of the couch and wrapped it around her shoulders. "This should help keep you warm until I get a fire started."

Leah caught my arm to keep me from rising. "I didn't get a chance to thank you before." She cupped the side of my face, caressing my cheekbone with her thumb. "Thank you…for coming to get me."

"Leah, I will always come for you. You are my…" *Mate.* I swallowed the word, leaned forward, and placed a kiss on her forehead. "I'll go put on some clothes, then we'll take a look at your hand and ankle and see about getting you something to eat."

"Okay." She pulled the ends of the blanket tighter to her chest, then settled farther into the cushions.

"I'll be right back." I padded down the hall and into the bedroom to tug on a pair of jeans and a T-shirt. Not exactly an outfit for a date. She'd already seen me naked, hadn't seemed unimpressed, so I was beyond worrying about my appearance. I was more concerned about how she'd view me as a caring mate.

Once dressed, I snatched a pillow off the bed, then made a quick stop in the bathroom to grab the first aid kit. When I returned to the living room, Leah had her eyes closed and appeared to be dozing. After what she'd been through, getting a little sleep was the best thing for her. Moving as quietly as possible, I retrieved several pieces of chopped wood from the stack I kept outside on the deck. A few minutes later, I'd coaxed a fire to life inside the fireplace.

I grabbed the plastic kit off the kitchen countertop where I'd left it. I sat on the end of the coffee table, content to watch Leah while she slumbered.

"Hey." She peered at me through half-lidded eyes. "Sorry I fell asleep."

"Not a problem. Now that you're awake, I'd like to

take a look at your hand and ankle." I motioned for her to shift sideways, then gently lifted her leg so it draped across my lap.

"Hand first." I untied the makeshift knot and removed the scrap of material she'd used from her shirt. I tore open an antiseptic wipe and began cleaning her palm.

Leah winced and jerked her hand.

"Sorry, almost done." I removed the last of the dried blood, glad to see the cut wasn't deep. After covering it with a Band-Aid, I switched my attention to her foot. "I'll try to be gentle, but this is going to hurt."

"Not the first time I've twisted my ankle… Go ahead," she said.

I untied her laces, slowly easing the boot off her foot and peeling off her sock. I touched the tender area, trying to assess if it was broken. I'd have Mitch X-ray her foot when I took her home to make sure.

She groaned and gripped the armrest with her good hand. "How bad is it?"

"Looks like a sprain."

"Guess I'll be limping at work for a few days. Mitch ought to love that." Her attempt at humor didn't change the distress reflected in her gaze.

"Let's put some ice on it and see if we can get the swelling to go down." I lifted her leg, scooted out of the way, and set the pillow underneath her foot. I made a quick trip to the kitchen and filled a resealable bag with ice. After grabbing a hand towel and two bottles of water out of the refrigerator, I returned to the living room. "Thought you might be thirsty." I twisted the cap off one bottle and handed it to her.

"Thanks." She took a long swig and rested the bottle in her lap.

I returned to my seat on the table, then wrapped the bag of ice in the towel and placed it on her foot. I had plenty of questions but figured they could wait until after I'd fed Leah. "Is there anything else I can get you before I go out and throw some steaks on the grill?"

"Food can wait." She grabbed my hand to keep me from leaving. "We need to talk."

Hearing her say the words no male ever wanted to hear was worse than getting kicked in the gut.

CHAPTER EIGHT

LEAH

I snuggled deeper into the blanket Bryson had wrapped around my shoulders and watched him disappear down a hallway in search of clothes. Up until recently, I hadn't been sure what I was going to do with my life, whether or not I'd make Ashbury my permanent home. I'd been trying to put my past with Caleb behind me but realized all I'd been doing was hiding. I hadn't been living, not until I'd met Bryson.

I'd been musing through the troubling thoughts, my body exhausted from the day's events. I'd closed my eyes only to open them a short time later to find Bryson watching me with the same intensity I'd seen in the eyes of his bear.

At first, discovering he could transform into an animal had been a little unsettling. Okay, it had bordered on massively disturbing. But now that I'd had some time to process the information, I realized it didn't change the way I felt about him. According to Mitch, there was an unspoken code that prevented shifters from sharing the details of their existence with humans. Maybe it was misplaced hope, but the fact that Bryson had come for me, risked exposing his animal to me, had to mean something, didn't it? Only people they trusted were ever made aware of the truth.

I didn't want to lose that trust and knew I needed to tell him about Caleb. There'd been a few times over the last couple of weeks that I'd tried, but every time I opened my mouth to speak, my courage vanished. I'd worried how he'd react after hearing about my past drama. Drama I'd thought was behind me and had resurfaced when Caleb showed up at my brother's house—the one place I'd thought I'd be safe.

Would Bryson change his mind about our steadily growing relationship and decide I wasn't worth the trouble? No matter what happened next, whether he was willing to accept my troubled past or call Mitch and tell him to come and get me, I owed him the truth.

I hadn't missed his flinch when I took his hand and told him we needed to talk.

"Okay." There was trepidation in his voice as he settled back on the edge of the coffee table facing me.

I took a sip of water, wishing it was something stronger to dull the pain of what might come next. "I haven't been completely truthful with you. I need to tell you the real reason I left California and moved out here to live with Mitch." Staring at my lap made it easier to continue. "I'd been dating a guy named Caleb, and about six months ago, I broke it off with him. Only he refused to accept that the relationship had ended." I ran my finger up and down the side of the plastic bottle.

"A few weeks after I refused to return his calls, he started stalking me. He wouldn't leave me alone and kept showing up where I worked, sometimes making a scene. It got so bad that I almost lost my job and had to get a restraining order. Not that it did any good. Several days afterward, he started parking in the lot near my apartment. That's when I realized he wasn't ever going to leave me alone."

"Is that when you decided to move here?" Bryson clasped my free hand with both of his.

The warmth from his touch, the support I recognized in his gaze, gave me the strength to continue. "Not quite. I finally broke down and told my mom what was going on." I hadn't wanted my mother to worry, so I'd kept the truth from her at first. We were close, and I didn't like keeping secrets from her. "She, of course, told Mitch, who talked me into staying with him for a while."

I'd wanted to handle the problem myself, not dump it on my family. At the time, I'd regretted my decision to confide in my mother, until Mitch showed up on my doorstep the next day. I'd never been so happy to see my older brother, but it had taken every persuasive skill I possessed to convince him not to go after Caleb.

"I'm glad he did." Bryson used the pad of his thumb to wipe away the tears cascading down my cheek. "Otherwise, I never would have found you."

Confused by his statement, I asked, "Don't you mean met me?"

"Yeah." Bryson nodded, though I got the impression it was more for my benefit than his. "Tell me what happened today?"

His encouragement made it easier to continue. "Mitch and I worked late last night, so he gave me the day off. I was looking forward to our date, had too much time on my hands, and decided to go for a hike."

"You were looking forward to tonight?" Bryson grinned and sat a little straighter.

"Yes." It always amazed me how such a big, tough-acting guy could be so adorable. Thinking about all that cuteness had images of him naked blazing a heated trail through my mind. My stomach fluttered; my concentration wavered. If I lost my focus, I wasn't going to be able to finish my explanation.

"Anyway, when I returned, I found Caleb banging on

the door and screaming my name. I refused to leave with him and ran back into the woods, hoping I could hide long enough for him to give up, then find my way to Gabe's place." So many things had gone wrong with my plan. I swallowed hard, trying to keep the fear I'd felt earlier from slipping into my voice. "Once I was sure Caleb was gone, I headed for Gabe's again. I wasn't paying attention to where I was going, tripped, and hurt my ankle. Not long after that, you showed up."

Now that Bryson knew everything, I was back to staring at my lap, where, surprisingly, he kept his hand wrapped around mine.

"Leah." Bryson's gentle squeeze drew my gaze to his. A genuine gaze filled with nothing but sincerity. "I don't care what happened in your past. All I care about is you being here with me." He paused as if searching carefully for his next words. "I haven't been totally honest with you either. There's something I should have told you, but I was afraid you wouldn't want to have anything to do with me after you found out."

"Well, I already know you can shift into a gigantic bear." After discovering that tidbit, what else could he have neglected to share with me? "Whatever it is, you can tell me. I'm not going anywhere."

He glanced at my ankle with an insinuating smile. We both knew there was no way I'd be able to hobble, hop, or drag myself all the way to my brother's house.

"That's not what I meant. Now tell me."

He licked his lips, the nervousness back in his gaze. "When Mitch was explaining about shifters, did he tell you about mates?"

I slowly nodded, curious why he was asking and what it had to do with what he'd been keeping from me. "Yes. He said that it was a destined match, that their animal side immediately recognized their life partner."

"What else did he tell you?" Bryson asked.

"That the bond between mates was permanent, even if

one of them was human." I tapped my chin trying to remember everything my brother had told me during my semi-drunken state. "Oh, and that their children will always be shifters, most likely taking on the animal traits of their father. Unless the father is human, then the mother's animal is predominant." The night Mitch explained what he knew about the shifter world, he'd been explicit in his details about that particular subject.

"What does that have to do with—"

"Leah," Bryson interrupted. "You're my mate."

I gasped, releasing a nervous laugh. "Whoa, that wasn't what I expected." *Not even close.* Had my brother already known about my connection to Bryson? Is that why he'd gone into such detail when he explained everything he knew about them? Was that why he'd encouraged me to go out with Bryson. And, more importantly, if what I suspected was true, was I going to strangle him for keeping it from me?

I must have been sitting there with my mouth hanging open longer than I thought, because Bryson squeezed my hand again to get my attention. "Leah, please say something."

"I… This is…"

"I know it's a lot to process," he said.

That is an understatement. I had more questions but started with the easy one first. "How long have you known?"

"From the moment I met you." Red seeped across his cheeks and he guiltily bowed his head.

Okay, so the immediate thing was true and everything about Bryson's curious behavior made sense. Because I was human, he must have assumed I didn't know anything about his world. It explained his aggressive behavior toward other guys and the reason he was taking things slow.

"I'm sorry I didn't tell you sooner. I'll understand if you don't want to have anything more to do with me and want to go back to your brother's house." Even when faced with the possibility of losing his mate, losing me, he put my wants and needs first. I was warmed by his honesty, his honorable effort to insist I make my own decision about the future of our relationship. It was touching, and so damned sexy.

Did I really want to walk away from him? Was I going to continue allowing my self-doubt and the events of my past to influence my future?

So what if he could transform into a bear. Was that really such a bad thing? He was still the same guy I was falling in love with before I found out about his animal.

If our future included children, which I hoped it did, would I be okay with raising little ones who could change into cubs? I remembered the little boy who'd turned into a wolf pup in my lap, and the harmless way he'd licked my face. Once I'd worked through my shock, I'd actually had fun playing with him.

I searched Bryson's expectant gaze, saw nothing but caring, and had my answer. If I was his mate, and we were truly meant to be together, then there was no reason not to do what I'd been wanting to do since our very first kiss. Ignoring the painful jolt to my ankle, I launched myself forward and straddled his lap, the towel and bag of ice plopping on the floor.

Shocked, Bryson reached for my hips. "What do you think you're doing?"

I pressed a finger against his lips. "I don't want to go back to my brother's place. I'd much rather stay here with you." I skimmed my hands along his broad shoulders, nestling them in the short hairs at his nape. "I want you to show me what being a mate entails."

BRYSON

Leah was going to fucking kill me. She'd surprised me

71

when she climbed on my lap, rubbed against my straining cock, and told me to show her what it meant to be a mate.

Thrilled by her acceptance, my heart thrummed. My bear, tired of being suppressed by my need to take things slow, surged close to the surface, pushing me to make her ours. Self-control went only so far when you were a dominant male and her request, the scent of her arousal, was a taunt I couldn't resist. "Leah, I…" A low, appreciative growl rumbled from my chest. My restraint slipped, and I sought her lips, a hard kiss filled with all the passion I possessed.

I coaxed the seam of her mouth, soliciting a whimper and possessively gaining access, our tongues tangling. I wanted to explore every one of her lush curves, then remembered her injured ankle. I'd give anything to make love to her, to be inside her, but her health and seeing to her needs took precedence.

I pulled back from the kiss, breathing raggedly, and pressed my forehead to hers. "We need to stop. You're hurt, and it's my responsibility to take care of you."

Leah tipped her head back, her eyes glistening with desire. "Is taking care of my needs part of being a mate?" She bit the side of her lip, making it hard to focus.

"Yes," I growled, wondering where she was going with this.

"Good, because I have a need to be in your bed." She squirmed, putting even more pressure on my erection, then had the audacity to smirk when I groaned.

Though Leah's playful, wanton behavior was a part of her I'd never seen before, the male in me highly approved. My bear found it appealing as well and rumbled with excitement, urging me to comply with her request. I still had reservations, was worried about her welfare, and asked, "Leah, are you sure?"

"Uh-huh," she said, wiggling again.

I got to my feet, bracing her ass with my arm and hoisting her along with me. Leah cupped my face and began kissing me. Damn female. I wanted to get down the hall but couldn't see where I was going and stopped.

"Taking too long." She nipped my chin, then giggled when I bumped against the wall trying to reach the bedroom quicker.

I finally made it inside the room, no thanks to Leah and her distracting assault. I placed her on top of the comforter, then carefully settled between her spread thighs.

She tugged at my shirt. "Clothes need to come off."

I grabbed her wrists, pinning them with one hand over her head.

"What the…" She pulled against my grip and frowned.

"Leah, slow down."

"Please. I want this, need this. My past…"

"Is in the past." If she needed reassurances, I would damn well make sure she had them. I couldn't undo what Caleb had put her through, but I could make her feel safe, show her how important she was to me. "I will give you everything you need, only slower, so we don't make your ankle worse." I grazed her cheek with my thumb. "Let me take care of you."

Some of the tension eased from her body. "Okay."

It was my turn for teasing, and I didn't waste any time drawing her into a kiss. A hungry kiss filled with all the passion I possessed. A kiss that elicited soft moans and had me wanting more. I'd been dying to see her naked for days and wanted the clothes between us gone as much as she did.

Releasing her wrists, I leaned back on my haunches and pulled my T-shirt over my head, then helped her off with hers. Eager to touch her creamy flesh, I extended a claw and sliced through the material at the front of her bra, exposing her luscious mounds.

"Bryson." Leah gave me an admonishing glare and slipped the remnants of her bra off her shoulders.

"I'll buy you another one," I said, knowing I'd be lying

if I told her I felt bad about the unusable condition of her undergarment. I silenced any further arguments by suckling a nipple into my mouth. While I worked the tip with my tongue, I skimmed her belly, running a finger underneath the waistband of her pants and undoing the button.

When I offered her other breast the same attention, she arched her back giving me better access. At the same time, I pushed down the zipper, working my hand between the fabric and her skin.

I slipped my finger through her soft curls, then made slow circles on her sex until she was gasping and digging her nails into my shoulders. Spreading her folds, I pushed a finger inside her. After several slow thrusts, I added another finger and continued the steady torment, enjoying the way she bucked against my ministrations.

"Please, I…" She pushed at the waistband of her pants, frantically trying to remove them.

"Let me help." I withdrew my hand, then eased her jeans, along with her panties, down her legs, careful not to jar her injured foot. The swelling around her ankle had diminished a little, but it still had to be causing her pain. I was assailed by a new wave of guilt, felt as if I was about to take advantage of her, instead of seeing to her needs.

She saw the direction of my gaze and grabbed a loop on the front of my jeans. "Don't even think about changing your mind." Determination flitted across her face. She jerked me forward, forcing me to brace my arms on either side of her to keep from falling on top of her.

"Have you always been such a bossy little thing?" I grinned and nibbled her earlobe.

"I know what I want, and right now, I want my mate." She made fast work of unzipping my pants and shoving them down my hips.

Mate. I loved hearing the proclamation, the possessiveness in her tone. Who was I to deny her what she wanted? I wanted to be inside her, skin to skin, and unencumbered by fabric. I rolled to the side and shed the remainder of my clothes, taking the time to commit her naked perfection to memory.

I covered her once again, wedging my hips between her legs and reveling in the feel of her heated skin. I left a trail of tender kisses, starting with her breast and ending with her lips.

"Stop teasing," she groaned, then dug her uninjured foot into the back of my thigh.

I chuckled against the crook of her neck, the place I would one day place my claiming mark. After reaching between us, I guided my cock to her opening, then slowly eased inside her, taking my time, allowing her to adjust to my size. Once fully seated, I began to thrust, finding a steady rhythm to push her closer to the edge.

"Bryson, I..." Her nails bit into the flesh on my back, and I knew she was close.

A few hard pumps and she toppled over the edge, screaming my name and shuddering through her orgasm. Several more thrusts, my body tightened, and I growled through my own release. I collapsed on top of her, our bodies slick with sweat, our breathing irregular.

Once I had the strength to move, I rolled to the side, taking her with me and making sure to keep her injured foot on top of my legs.

Her eyes were closed, but I could tell she wasn't sleeping. A glimmer of self-doubt had worked its way into my mind. What if I hadn't met her expectations? What if she'd changed her mind about being my mate? "Leah, are you okay?"

"Is it always going to be like that?" She opened her eyes and smiled. "Because that was incredible."

I startled awake to find Leah tucked against my side and using my shoulder as a pillow. I rubbed my nose in her hair, savoring her scent. As much as I would have enjoyed waking her for another round of lovemaking, I wanted her to get some rest.

Though daylight was only a few hours away, it was still dark outside, the sky glittered with fading stars. Even though the bedroom window faced the side of the house, it wasn't hard to detect outside noises. It didn't hurt that I had enhanced hearing or that sounds carried in this area. When I heard the engine of not one but two vehicles approaching the house, I realized what had disturbed my sleep. Shortly after the motors stopped, doors slammed and footsteps crunched on the gravel drive.

"Where do you think you're going?" I heard Nick's deep, gravelly voice and assumed he must be here to return my truck.

"Don't you think we should check on them, make sure Leah is all right?" I imagined Mandy with her hands on her hips, glaring at her mate.

"No. You should know it's never a good idea to mess with a shifter when he's alone with his mate. Especially if the shifter is a big, grumpy bear." There was humor in Nick's tone, leading me to believe he was certain I was listening.

"Well, I'm going to check…" Mandy squealed. "Darn it, Nick, put me down. You can't keep throwing me over your shoulder and carrying me around like a sack of potatoes."

"Says who?" He chuckled.

"And stop pinching my backside."

"But it's such a nice… Hey, what was that for?" The rest of their conversation was cut off by the sound of a slamming door. A few seconds later, one of the engines roared to life, then faded into the distance.

Friends didn't get any better than Nick, and later, when I called him to find out what happened to Caleb, I'd thank him for not interrupting my time with Leah.

CHAPTER NINE

BRYSON

I stood inside the empty resort cabin, watching through partially drawn shades as the red car with California license plates and Caleb behind the wheel came to a stop next to Leah's vehicle. The building was located at the secluded end of the property and wasn't scheduled to be rented for another two days. Plenty of time to take care of the male who'd made my mate's life hell.

Leah hadn't been happy when I'd told her what I planned to do. It had taken some convincing and a bout of lovemaking to get her to remain at my place with Mandy while the rest of us took care of the problem strutting toward the porch with a condescending smirk on his face. My bear wanted to rip him to shreds and was pushing me hard to allow a shift.

I had to admit the idea was tempting, but I had to consider what my actions would do to Leah. The shifter world could be dangerous, sometimes cruel and deadly. Though I accepted that part of my life, I never wanted Leah to see it. And I would do whatever it took to protect her and shield her from it.

Personally, I didn't have a problem with hurting the human to teach him a lesson, but my sweet, caring mate would. I couldn't, however, let Caleb walk away, not without ensuring that he never bothered her or any other female again.

Caleb had broken her restraining order. The matter should have been turned over to local law enforcement, yet it didn't guarantee he'd stay out of her life. I didn't want her to spend another minute dealing with the repercussions or worrying about his reappearance. After a lengthy discussion with Reese, Nick, and Preston, we'd come up with a better plan. A plan that, so far, Caleb was making easy.

After everything I'd learned about the male and the trouble he'd gone to to find Leah, I assumed he wasn't going to leave without seeing her again. And I'd been right.

Shortly after my friends arrived at Mitch's to help with the search, they'd confirmed via scent that the male who gone after Leah was also the owner of the car. Preston had parked out of sight, waited for the male to return, then followed him—straight to the lodge. He'd booked a room using his real name and confirming Mitch's suspicions that it was Caleb.

I wanted him out of Leah's life permanently, but I couldn't go to the lodge and confront him. With a little help and some strategic planning, we'd hoped to lure him to the cabin, where I'd be able to confront him and convince him that his continued pursuit of my mate was a bad, possibly lethal idea.

When Berkley had delivered a note to Caleb supposedly from Leah, he had no idea he'd be meeting with me instead of her. "Hello, Caleb," I said, walking out onto the porch.

Caleb stopped with his hand on the railing, a foot on the lower step. "Who the fuck are you?" He glanced behind me. "And where is Leah?"

"She's not coming." I clenched my fists, urging my

claws and my animal to remain hidden.

Caleb narrowed his gaze and scowled. "And why not?"

"Because she's my mate and no longer your concern."

"Look, bud, I don't know what a mate is, but Leah belongs with me." He removed his foot from the step. "And you're going to tell me where she is."

The arrogant male obviously didn't know it was never a good idea to challenge a dominant, and now highly irritated, bear. Maybe I'd be doing everyone in his life a favor by getting rid of him. "No, I'm not." I took an intimidating step forward.

Before I could decide if he was worth the trouble, one of the resort's trucks pulled into the driveway. Preston and Mitch got out, which meant Reese and Nick were somewhere nearby in their wolf forms, just in case things turned nasty.

Caleb turned from the porch to face the new arrivals. "What are they doing here?"

Mitch didn't give me a chance to answer. "So you're the asshole who's been making my sister's life hell." There was no missing the anger in his voice.

"And you must be the interfering brother. The one who thought he could keep Leah away from me."

Mitch might be a few inches shorter than Caleb, but I was certain he could easily make up the difference with anger if the two of them got into a fight. Hopefully, though, if the plan went the way we'd discussed, none of us would have to lift a finger against Caleb.

"You're only half correct." Mitch cracked his knuckles. "Leah doesn't want to have anything to do with you."

"You're wrong. She just needs a little convincing is all." Caleb jutted out his chin, too stupid to realize his arrogance wasn't going to help him.

"If you're not going to let me talk to Leah, then what am I doing here?" Caleb asked.

"You could say we've planned an intervention of sorts," Preston said, taking a position next to Mitch.

Caleb sneered. "Let me guess. You think if you beat the hell out of me that I'm going to rethink the error of my ways and walk away from her." His bravado wavered, his fear-filled stench wafted through the air, and he inched closer to his car.

By ignoring the mandates of the restraining order, Caleb had already proven his disregard for following the law. I had a feeling no amount of physical persuasion was going to change his mind either, so it was time for part two of the plan.

Sharing the existence of our shifter nature with humans was frowned up except under special, usually life-threatening, circumstances. After a lengthy discussion and analyzing all the pros and cons with my friends, we'd determined this was one of those situations.

There was always the risk that Caleb, after working through his terror, might decide to share what he'd seen with members of his family or friends. Luckily, Reese and Preston had some retired military buddies who were more than happy to keep an eye on Caleb.

I didn't ask how they planned to manage the task but got the impression they'd do whatever was necessary to ensure the male was no longer a threat to Leah or our kind.

"You're going to leave the resort, leave Colorado, and, more specifically, leave Leah alone. *Forever.*" I toed off my boots, decided he wasn't worth ruining a good pair of pants and a shirt, so they followed next.

"Are you planning to fight me naked? Afraid I might get blood on your clothes?" Caleb's face lost all color.

"No fighting, but blood will be drawn if you ever show your face around here again." I lumbered down the remaining steps, then took my time transforming into my bear. I made sure Caleb heard every bone snap. Saw his horrified expression as he watched my snout grow, my claws elongate, and my teeth protrude.

Not all human minds were capable of accepting the

unbelievable. To them, a shifter's existence was outside their realm of reality. Judging by the ever-increasing wet spot on Caleb's crotch, I was convinced he fell into that category.

With a satisfied smirk, Mitch returned to Preston's truck and retrieved the suitcase that belonged to Caleb. Shortly after Berkley had called to tell me the male was on his way to the cabin, she'd let herself into his room with a master key. She'd packed all his belongings, checked him out and gave the case to Preston.

"Keep…keep…keep it away from me," Caleb shrieked and waved his hands wildly as he backed toward his car.

"Unless you want him to show up in your home in the middle of the night and do to you what bears do best, I'd suggest you leave my sister alone." Mitch opened the rear door of Caleb's car and tossed the case inside. "Never show your face around here again."

"You people are nuts." Caleb bumped into the frame, then spun, patting the hood on his way to the driver's side of the vehicle. "No bitch is worth this."

I growled at the nasty comment directed at my mate and padded a few steps forward.

"Fuck." Caleb couldn't move quickly enough to get behind the wheel and peel out of the driveway.

Mitch glanced over at Preston, who was leaning against the front of his truck. "You think he'll tell anybody what he saw?"

I shifted back into my human form and grinned. "What, that he saw a grown man turn into a bear, then threaten to eat him?"

"Guess not." Mitch laughed.

"Thanks for your help." I returned to the porch to put on my clothes. Once I slipped on my boots, I headed for Leah's car. "Now if you don't mind, I have a mate I need to get back to."

CHAPTER TEN

LEAH

I stared at the thick wall of trees outside the passenger window of Bryson's truck. It had been three days since he'd gone off to meet with Caleb, leaving me a worried wreck. A meeting I was relieved to hear later hadn't ended in bloodshed. While the guys had been off ensuring I'd never be bothered again, Mandy had volunteered to stay with me at Bryson's house. I had a feeling she was there more to keep me from leaving than to keep me company.

Luckily, she'd done a good job helping me pass the time by distracting me with humorous stories about her friendship with Berkley and growing up in Ashbury. I'd discovered, to my frustrating dismay, that prior to the night Bryson had rescued me in the forest, everyone at the lodge had learned that I was his mate, including my traitorous brother. She'd been happy to answer my questions about the shifter world and even informed me that Nick was part wild wolf.

She'd made of point of letting me know that when Bryson was in protective-bear mode, no one was willing to mess with him. Well, no one except me. With me, he was a total teddy bear. I smiled, remembering how Mandy had used air quotes to emphasize the teddy bear part.

"Bryson." Gazing at his handsome profile took my breath away, and I still couldn't believe he was my mate.

"Yeah?" He glanced in my direction and smiled.

"Are you going to tell me where we're going?" It was the third time I'd asked the question in the last half hour since we'd left his house.

"Maybe."

Great, we were back to his elusive answers. "You've been waiting on me for three days now. My foot is healed." Well, mostly healed. It was a little tender, but the limp was hardly noticeable. I'd even been able to wear shoes without any problems. "I'm sure my brother needs my help, and don't they expect you back at the lodge?"

"Mitch said he had it covered, and I have a bunch of vacation time saved up." He took one hand off the steering wheel, reached for mine, and squeezed. "Taking care of you is important."

"Arguing with you isn't going to do me any good, is it?" It didn't mean I wasn't going to keep trying.

"Nope." We'd been driving for a half hour and already passed the main exit to Hanford, the only other city besides Ashbury that was close to the resort. He slowed the truck, then cranked the wheel to the right and drove onto an old worn and rutted road. It wound through a thick expanse of aspen and spruce, similar to the area I'd seen the day he'd taken me to the falls. Today's trip didn't include a lunch basket, so I assumed we weren't going on another picnic.

"We're here," he said, pulling into a drive that came to a stop in front of a two-story cabin-style home.

"Where is here?" My question went unanswered because Bryson was already out of the truck, his door clicking shut. In several long strides, he'd circled to my side of the vehicle and was holding the door open.

He swept me into his arms before the tip of my shoe

reached the gravel. I was glad I'd chosen to wear jeans rather than the knee-length black skirt that had been my first choice. Otherwise, I'd be flashing my underwear and the color I felt blazing across my cheeks would be a lot brighter. "I am capable of walking." I draped my arms around his shoulders.

"I know," Bryson murmured close to my ear. "I like carrying you."

Not new information since he hadn't let me do a lot of walking after making me his houseguest.

As soon as we reached the stairs leading up to a wraparound porch, an elderly couple emerged from inside the house. Both had medium brown hair with a sprinkling of gray. The man was tall with a build similar to Bryson's. The woman had a sturdy frame and rounded cheeks and stood about a foot shorter.

"Leah, I'd like you to meet Glenda and Richard, my mom and dad." He lowered me to my feet, keeping one arm wrapped around my waist.

Mom and dad. Meeting his parents was a big deal, one I would have appreciated getting a heads-up for. If I could've punched Bryson, I would have. But since he had me pinned to his side and at a disadvantage, the most I could do was pinch him below the ribs. "You could have told me," I whispered through gritted teeth.

Undaunted by my precursor to retribution, he grinned.

With a warning glare, I slipped from his grasp and held out my hand. "It's nice to…" Before I could finish, I found myself in Glenda's solid embrace. It was a good thing I had some additional flesh on my bones; otherwise, breathing would have been difficult.

After releasing me, she did the same with Bryson. "Your mate is lovely," she said, then smacked him. "Why haven't you claimed her yet?"

"Mom," Bryson groaned and rubbed his arm. "Remember the talk we had about discussing personal things that aren't any of your business?"

Glenda tsked and waved her hand dismissively in his face. "Leah is family now, so that doesn't count."

"What is claiming?" It wasn't a term I was familiar with, but I was sure it had something to do with being a shifter. And if it had anything to do with sex, then we'd covered that area more than once since the night Bryson had informed me I was his mate. I crossed my arms, curious to hear what he had to say and find out why I hadn't heard about it until now.

Richard, who had yet to enter the conversation, appeared amused. He took my hand and aimed me toward the house. "I'll bet you have a lot of questions. Why don't we go inside and discuss them over some of Glenda's homemade lemonade?"

I heard Bryson groan and glanced behind me, noting his discomfort. "Thanks, I'd like that," I said, giving Richard a beaming smile. It seemed retribution was arriving sooner than I'd hoped.

BRYSON

I didn't blame Leah for being irritated with me. I probably should have told her about the trip to meet my parents. I'd learned a long time ago that no amount of forewarning could prepare anyone for the force of nature that was my mother. The female was outspoken, incorrigible, and lacked any concept of respecting the personal boundaries of her children.

I was seated comfortably next to Leah on a long, cushioned sofa. Or at least as comfortable as a male could get while under his mother's scrutinizing gaze. After pouring us drinks, she plopped down next to my father on a two-seated sectional positioned across from us.

"So, what is claiming?" Leah asked again, apparently not going to give up until someone gave her the information she wanted.

My mother made the best lemonade, but my mate's question caught me in the middle of enjoying a sip, and I coughed.

My father chuckled, then slid a coaster under his glass before setting it on the coffee table between us. "Son, would you like to explain it to her, or would you rather have your mother do it?"

"I'd prefer it if we didn't discuss it at all," I snapped, my voice still raspy after nearly choking.

"Well, I want grandchildren." My mother pinned me with a furious glare and threw her hands up in the air. "I could be waiting forever or end up long dead if it was left up to your brother and his mate. You'd think with both of them being engineers that they'd have figured out how things work by now."

My mother already knew that my brother, Matt, and his mate were involved in their careers and putting off starting a family for a few more years.

She took my father's hand and smiled at me. "You were conceived during our claiming, so…"

"Mom," I growled. "Too. Much. Information." I scowled at Leah, whose suppressed giggle wasn't helping the situation.

"Don't be silly. It's a natural part of our world, and Leah has a right to know," my mother said.

I wasn't a prude, but as honest and straightforward as my mother was, any explanation she'd give would include graphic details. I hadn't realized I was squirming until Leah placed her hand on my thigh and took pity on me. "It's okay. Bryson can explain it to me later when we get back to our place."

Had she really said "our place"? Though I'd done some hinting, we hadn't discussed her moving in with me. I was waiting for her to be at ease with the idea of being my mate before I made it official by claiming her.

"Are you sure?" I searched her gaze for any indication that I'd misconstrued her meaning.

"Very sure."

I couldn't suppress my feelings any longer. "I love you, Leah," I said, then pulled her onto my lap and kissed her. The kind of possessive kiss that shouldn't be shared with an audience, let alone my parents. And for once, I didn't care.

"It won't be long now." My mother's cheery voice cut through my euphoric haze and killed all thoughts of seducing my mate.

Confused, Leah asked, "What won't be long?"

"Grandbabies, of course." Beaming with satisfaction, she winked and reached for her lemonade.

"Dad, can't you do something with her?" I asked.

My father, the one person I always relied on, simply wiggled his eyebrows. "I could, but making out with your mother is a little inappropriate in front of company, don't you think?"

CHAPTER ELEVEN

BRYSON

"So, are you going to do it or not?" Leah asked, then bent forward and nipped my lower lip. What started out as a playful attempt to snatch one of her freshly baked muffins ended up with us in bed naked and her straddling my hips.

By "doing it," I knew she meant claiming her. And once again, I found myself frustrated with my mother. I loved the female, was grateful she'd given birth to me, but wished she understood the meaning of TMI.

Now, thanks to my mother's unwanted honesty, Leah was constantly asking me to take the next and final step in the mating process. I'd put it off for over a week because I wanted her to be sure, but my excuses were starting to sound lame, even to me.

The other factor weighing heavily on my mind was Leah's lack of enhanced healing. I knew Mandy had survived the claiming bite with Nick without any problems, but there was a significant difference in tooth size between his wolf and my bear.

My animal's incisors, even when I extended them in my

human form, were large. Claiming required a bite. A bite that had to be painful and would leave a scar. Hence the claiming mark that all other males in my world would recognize and know Leah was taken.

My bear, on the other hand, was in complete agreement with Leah. He wanted to see his mark on her body, to know she belonged to us, and that no male would dare come near her afterward.

"No." I was interrupted by a bark. Bear, who'd been staying with us, rose on his hind legs and pawed the comforter where it hung over the side of the bed. He'd had another incident with a porcupine, and Leah had volunteered to take care of him for the next few days while Nick tracked down the prickly animal and found a good place to relocate him.

"He probably needs to go out." Leah squirmed to get off me.

"He can wait, but I can't." I gripped her hips and rolled her onto her back, positioning the tip of my cock near her wet and inviting entrance.

Since Mandy mentioned that the dog liked to sleep on their bed, it was probably the reason for his interruption. I wasn't in the mood to share. "Bear, go lie down," I ordered, then grinned when he groaned and headed for the bed Leah had made out of blankets for him on the floor in the corner.

I snagged her nipple into my mouth, sucked long and hard, then teased the tip with my tongue.

"Not fair," she moaned, digging her fingers into my scalp and arching to give me more access.

Not fair was my inner turmoil, the need to make her mine, yet I feared I might hurt her. I wanted to be buried deep inside her, to feel her writhing beneath me. I slowly inched my cock forward, taking my time, savoring every sensation.

"Bryson...please."

I knew that tone, knew what she wanted, but I wasn't ready to give it to her. Instead, I pumped slowly, steadily leading her toward that pleasurable climatic peak, but refusing to give her that final push that would send her over the edge.

"Fine, if you won't, then I will," she said.

Comprehension, the knowledge that her words had a deeper meaning, didn't come fast enough. Leah dug her heels into the backs of my thighs, clutched me tightly, then sank her teeth into the fleshy muscle of my right shoulder.

"Leah." I groaned, unable to keep my bear from responding to her challenge by elongating my teeth. Instinctively, I bit the spot I'd mentally marked the first time we'd made love. At the same time, I thrust into her hard and deep.

Leah screamed against my skin, her climax instantaneous. The taste of her blood mixed with her unique scent drove me over the edge. An animalistic growl tore from my throat. My body shook, quivering through the most intense orgasm I'd ever experienced. It left me drained and panting, with barely enough strength to retract my teeth and brace myself to keep from crushing her.

After my pounding pulse eased and my breathing returned to normal, I rolled the tip of my tongue over the bite on her shoulder and licked off the remnants of blood. "I can't believe you bit me."

"I love you with all my heart." She pressed a kiss to my cheek. "But you were taking too long."

"How did you know that a bite would trigger a claiming?" I asked.

She grinned. "You're not the only one who can ask people for advice."

"You talked about this, about us, with someone else?" Who had she talked to? I'd made Mandy and Berkley swear to secrecy about their role in helping me when I was dating Leah. That left Nick. I really didn't want to hurt the wolf, but if he'd been giving my mate sex advice, then we were going to have a problem.

"Yes. I consulted an expert." Leah giggled, appearing proud of her accomplishment.

"No," I groaned after realizing the culprit's identity. "Please don't tell me you talked to my mother."

"You'd be surprised what she knows."

No, I wouldn't, since my mother had happily shared her wisdom with her children and anyone else who would listen for years. On one hand, I was glad my mother approved of Leah and welcomed her into our family. On the other, I was dreading what their close relationship meant for me.

I couldn't decide if I wanted to throttle Leah for consulting my mother or torture her with sexual pleasure. Now that our bond was permanent and she was mine, the latter held limitless possibilities.

ABOUT THE AUTHOR

Rayna Tyler is an author of paranormal and sci-fi romance. She loves writing about strong sexy heroes and the sassy heroines who turn their lives upside down. Whether it's in outer space or in a supernatural world here on Earth, there's always a story filled with adventure.

Printed in Great Britain
by Amazon